Katha

Boys Don't Ride

Tull was starving.

Thunder had been rolling quietly around his stomach for the last hour or so.

Now, staring at the pulled down shutters of the school's canteen over the heads of five other students, he could actually hear the rumbling clearly above the noise the cluster of Year 12 boys at the front was making. He wondered whether the girl that stood between them and him could hear it, too.

She was half a head shorter than him, ergo half a head closer to his gargling intestines, but if she had noticed she was polite enough not to show it. Or maybe she was just too absorbed in balancing her various belongings. She was carrying an art folder as well as her PE bag in her right hand, while holding some kind of shoebox object in her left. He wondered how she was going to pick up her tray but another loud noise from his midriff interrupted his musings. It sent his cheeks blushing and he turned to look out of the window into the drab November grey.

The world outside had been doused in cold, slushy sleet that morning and he focused his attention on the starbursts of spray on the pane, trying hard not to be too aware of the girl's proximity, but even with his nose turned away he could still smell her.

She smelled good.

Not like most of the other six form girls who were followed around the corridors by wafts of obnoxious perfume but like a person who had showered that morning. Her short, very fair hair exuded the faint scent of apple, vanilla and cinnamon - like his mum's Christmas crumble. There was also something else, something more permanent, more fundamental, something he knew he should know but couldn't quite grasp that came with an almost unbearable yearning. Frustrated with not being able to identify it, he concentrated on the crumble aspect and his body promptly emitted another loud growl.

He turned back to see if she was looking at him yet. As he did he caught a glimpse of one of the boys in front who was stumbling backward that instant, threatening to crush her.

Just in time, Tull managed to put a protective arm around her personal space. He propped the intruder up with a flat palm between the shoulder blades and gave him a nudge forward.

"Careful, man, there are other people here," he heard himself say sternly.

He kept his arm up a while longer, hugging the air around her and suddenly became acutely aware of the force field that seemed to surround her. It was pushing against his skin, like the north of one magnet pushing the north of another. Bewildered he let his hand sink back to his side.

While the boy in front uttered a series of half hearted 'sorries', already heading into the canteen that had finally opened its gates, the girl glanced at Tull over her shoulder and mouthed a 'thank you'.

He could tell that surprise mixed itself into her gratitude once she'd laid eyes on him.

He knew that look.

It said that faces like his were not supposed to be nice or caring. They were supposed to be arrogant and condescending.

Though once thought that idea itself seemed so vain it made his cheeks burn with shame.

A second later they were swept along by the ravenous queue that had formed behind them and he immediately lost her in the hustle and bustle. For the fraction of a second, before he turned his attention to the business of selecting food, he contemplated her weird looks.

Her ever so slightly slanted green eyes that he would have expected to be blue to go with her almost white hair had sat left and right of a bridgeless, flattish and slightly lopsided nose, giving her an overall feline appearance. Two telltale scars running into the ill defined cupid's bow of her ragged lips had whispered *cleft palate baby* at him. In a weirdly raffish way she had still been quite pretty though.

Scrappy cat pretty.

Some kid bumped into him and he shook himself out of the reverie to begin inwardly debating meal choices in earnest. The hot food counter lured with offerings that warmed the stomach but hot lunches were almost twice the price of a baguette and it was the beginning of the month. Tull could never be sure whether his dad would already have topped up his school meals account or not and his own wallet was sitting on his desk at home. Having to leave a baguette at the till was infinitely less embarrassing than having to take a hot lunch plate, complete with extra gravy, back to the dinner ladies behind the counter, so at last a rubber bread stick filled with tuna glue and limp salad won the debate. He made his way to one of the tills with trepidation. His inkling proved right when the cashier shook her head as soon as Tull put his index finger onto the cashless payment scanner.

"Not enough credit, darling, you need to go to the machine and top up," she stated flatly.

He shrugged and grabbed the baguette.

"I'll take it back," he mumbled dejectedly.

Suddenly a pale hand touched him just below the elbow, exerting the lightest of pressure. It was dry, warm, a little calloused with short, ragged nails and bore serious strength underneath the mere brush of a touch. His skin appeared to be suckered towards it, nestling itself firmly into the rough palm.

"I'll put it on mine," the girl said quietly, "You can pay me back another time."

She detached and he found her face to see her smiling at him.

A tiny, close-lipped smile.

Their eyes made contact and in that shortest of moments he could see the kindred soul.

She'd been there, done that, bought the t-shirt.

She *knew* what it was like being this hungry and not having a penny to one's name.

She knew about absent fathers that sometimes paid and sometimes didn't. And about mothers who were present but refused to get involved once an agreement had been struck.

She knew.

~~~

Days later he was lying on his bed, watching a hairline crack in the ceiling slowly grow fainter as dusk advanced outside and thinking about her again.

She had paid, nodded at him curtly and then disappeared with her tray and all her belongings into the dinner hall, hardly giving him time to thank her or ask her name.

He'd managed to find her the next day to give back what he owed her. It had earned him another minimalist smile, another sharp nod, another missed opportunity to ask who she was. And that had been the end of the story.

Only it hadn't been.

He couldn't stop thinking about her, couldn't help but look out for her every day.

That random act of kindness, such a rarity in the jungle of an educational establishment, had humbled him. He wanted to know what kind of person would do that, what kind of person could be both so guarded and generous at the same time, what kind of person was behind those eyes that had understood so much so quickly. He wanted to know what the shoebox had been about, why her hands were so calloused, what shampoo she used to make her hair smell of Christmas, what that scent underneath had been and whether the scars to her lip itched sometimes when the weather was hot, the way his appendicitis one did. There was also the part of him that kept imagining what it would be like to kiss those jagged edged lips, whether it would change the feel of kissing significantly or not.

Those lips.

Mouthing 'thank you' at him.

He'd liked that.

He wanted them to do that again.

He dragged himself out of the daydream when he heard the faint clip clop of hooves through the shut window. He listened to their rhythm and tried to determine how many sets, how many horses there were in the road. Three, he reckoned, and they were hurrying at a fast walk, undoubtedly trying to get home before the light in the sky would fade completely.

He didn't get up to check though.

When they had first moved out to the edge of the city, years ago, after his parents had split, he had got properly excited every time riders went past the house. Rain or shine, he had run out of the front door and stood by the edge of the road to watch them go by. While other boys in his class had known every type of dinosaur, Tull had been able to recite all the horse colours by heart and would tell anyone who was prepared to listen the difference between a dark and a bright bay, between the chestnuts – golden, ginger and liver - between a piebald and a skewbald, a palomino and a cremello and between the many different types of grey.

Sometimes the riders had stopped and let him stroke a horse's soft nostril or pat it on the neck. Afterwards Tull would pester his mum for days to buy him a pony and later, when he understood better, to at least let him have lessons at the local riding school, just up the road. His mum would explain patiently time and time again that there was no money for such expensive activities and when Tull had finally plucked up the courage to ask his father he'd got the cliché answer his then ten-year-old self had already expected.

Riding, his father had stated categorically, was for girls. Little girls with rich parents and ponies called Jemima.

Undeterred, Tull had started saving up what little pocket money he received but by the time he'd finally managed to save up enough for one lesson, the riding school had shut down. The place had been a private yard ever since, riders still rode past his house but joining them one day had become even more unattainable than ever.

Little Tull had cried himself to sleep when he'd heard about the closure, taken his Equine Colour Chart off the wall, packed up his horse fact books and resigned himself to his fate as a non-rider. To this day, he still stopped at every horse field he came across and fed any occupant interested a handful of grass from the wayside but he had long given up on running out of the house to catch a glimpse.

As the sound of the riders ebbed away, a creak from the door hinges told him that the cat had pushed her head into the room. He turned to watch her pad stealthily across to the bed only to jump onto the mattress next to him with a loud, self announcing meow. She butted his hip with her forehead but Tull knew better than to pet her. The bundle of black and white fur he had rescued out of a bin years ago did not take kindly to being stroked. No matter how friendly her rubbing against him seemed he knew that upon the merest touch she'd pounce on his hand and dig her claws far enough into his flesh to draw blood. Her rules of engagement had always been clear. She could love him but under no circumstances was he to love her back. Tull took a deep breath and suppressed the urge to stroke her anyway.

Unattainable beings. Story of his life.

He swallowed hard and got up to see what the kitchen cupboard would yield for dinner.

~~~

"Right, I give up," Sue pushed her plate away and folded her arms on the table, "You haven't said more than two words to me in days. I am fully aware that I didn't give birth to a potential chat show host but this is ridiculous. Out with it. What are you moping about?"

"Boys don't mope, mum, boys brood."

Tull chased the last two pasta shells around his plate listening to his mum chuckle. It didn't last long though.

"Come on, Tull," she pleaded, "Don't shut me out. What's up?"

"There is this girl," he began answering half-heartedly while he carried on playing with his food.

"Uh-huh," his mum made one of her counsellor noises and Tull could feel himself getting annoyed already.

"Don't try and counsel me, mum."

"I'm not. I'm listening."

"I rest my case."

"Clever clogs."

"Now we're talking," Tull grinned sarcastically.

"Okay, so there is a girl," Sue stated with an ill disguised smile, "and you like her?"

"I don't know. I don't really know her. - She bought me lunch."

"Well, I like her already. So what did you talk about?"

"We didn't. That's all she did. Literally. I was…" he stopped himself before he would inadvertently rouse another discussion about his dad and the continuously erratic side of the lunch money arrangements and waved his fork dismissively, "It doesn't matter. Forget it. I don't really want to talk about it."

He skewered the last two *conchiglie* onto the prongs, put them in his mouth and got up to collect the dishes, still chewing.

"Leave it," his mum said taking the plates from his hands, "you did the cooking - and delicious it was, too, thank you very much - I'll do the washing up."

Tull nodded and made to leave the front room.

"And Tull?"

He turned to face her again. In the dim light of the single, chrome skirted bulb that hung over their little dining table she looked tired and old. Her silver streaked frizzy brown curls framed a heart shaped face with delicate features that normally looked a decade younger than she actually was but tonight she seemed to be made exclusively of hollow cheeks and sunken eye sockets.

"You're an exceptionally good-looking boy," she sighed, "And kind, too. If she's worth her salt she'll notice."

He smiled at his mother then, knowing that she would never understand if he told her that his stupid good looks were exactly the problem. He took a step towards her and retrieved the plates she was still clutching.

She looked down, frowning at her suddenly empty hands.

"What do you think you're doing?" she asked thinly.

"Tidying up," Tull jerked his head in direction of the settee, "You. Sofa. Now."

She didn't fight it and when Tull came back fifteen minutes later to wipe the table down, she was already fast asleep in front of the TV.

He put a blanket over her, switched the telly over to a programme he knew she'd watch if she was awake and left the room.

~~~

"Hey, stop staring at Lips, will ya? It's bordering on rude," Amelia nudged him hard in the ribs.

Tull jerked and took his eyes off the girl sitting on her own at the far corner table of the dinner hall, ear phones stuck in her ears, music player in hand, which she appeared to stop and start at regular intervals in between jotting something down on a piece of paper.

He looked around his own table, slightly disorientated.

There were eight of them. Amelia, Karla, Ben, Rosie, Nathan, Ed, Connor and Roland. Names and faces he'd known for years, saw every day, listened to endlessly, might even consider friends but, really, they were just other people.

People he didn't know and who didn't know him.

"What's going on?" Amelia's elbow made impact with his side once more and a broad grin spread across her overly made up face.

Tull turned to her, frowning deeply.

"What did you call her?"

"What? Lips?"

"That's really nasty," he scowled.

Amelia looked taken aback, pushing her lower lip out into a semi-pout that once upon a time had driven him crazy with lust. These days it just looked childish to him. Although no less kissable than before, he had to admit.

She was a good kisser, Amelia.

He'd shamelessly sampled her aptitude for tongue gymnastics at every opportunity for most of Year 12 but somehow, over the summer holidays they'd slowly stopped seeing each other. There had been no big break up scene, the same way there had never been an eligibly romantic getting-together-story. The previous Halloween Amelia, dressed as The Corpse Bride, had insisted that Tull's scraped-together, vaguely Victorian zombie outfit could be easily mistaken for a passable love interest and had simply pounced on him. It had been nice, so they'd kept it going but without much interaction aside from rolling tongues around in each other's mouths they'd both become increasingly bored over the months. Eventually, it had simply ended in a trickling demise of interest on both sides, culminating in a party at Ben's house where she'd gone to lavish her talents on the host instead. She had been doing so ever since.

"No it's not," she stated defensively, "That's her name. That's what everyone at mum's yard calls her. She don't mind. "

At the mentioning of the fact that Amelia's mother possessed a horse Tull felt a familiar stab of envy in his gut. While they'd been sort of going out he'd asked her a couple of times if they could go and see it one day. She had said 'sure' but nothing had ever come of it. Amelia didn't really do horses outside of bragging about her family owning one.

As if his comprehension was on time delay this morning, he suddenly understood what she'd just said and felt a smile spread across his face as the realisation hit him with all the force of a lightening bolt.

Horse. The smell. Underneath the crumble. It had been horse.

His eyes wandered back to the lone figure across the hall.

"Doesn't," he corrected Amelia with a distracted sigh, "She *doesn't* mind. – And I doubt it. What's her real name?"

"Liberty," Amelia answered sullenly, "You fancy *her*?"

He wanted to throttle her for the disbelief in her voice but instead he got up and smiled down at her.

"I don't know, yet. But I'm going to find out."

As he left their table he put himself in their shoes for a moment, observed himself swagger off confidently through their eyes. He wished it was real. He wished his mouth hadn't dried to Sahara level and that he wouldn't be able to hear all the seven oceans rushing in his ears.

What was it about this girl that intimidated him this much?

Why did she make him this nervous?

While he approached he watched her absent-mindedly pick up the Styrofoam cup she'd been sipping from, put it to her lips and then set it down without swallowing any liquid. Evidently it had run empty. His heart rate normalised a little then and he inwardly breathed a sigh of relief. At the very least he had a way in. He could offer to buy her another coffee. He had credit today.

She looked up when he reached her, frowned for a moment then dug the ear phones out of their habitat. He could hear the music pouring out ever so faintly. It was something familiar. Something ye-olde-worldy from his mum's record collection.

He could feel his face light up when he finally recognised the tune.

"Is that The Waterboys? It is, isn't it? It's Raggle Taggle Gypsy."

She nodded slowly before pushing pause on the player. The frown dissipated and an inscrutable mask took its place.

"What can I do for you, Tull?" she asked evenly.

He flinched in surprise, "You know my name?"

The frown came back as she held his gaze, mixed with a sceptical curl of the mouth.

"*Everyone* knows who you are."

"Not true," he stated as he sat down, being careful not to break eye contact even for a fraction of a second. He had her but he knew it was a tenuous connection at best. There was wariness in her eyes, a preparedness to jump up and run at the drop of a hat that made her appear even more like a cat than the mere felineness of her quirky facial features suggested. He could sense her tense up more and finally looked away, picking up her empty cup to play with it.

"They know my name," he said quietly, "but they haven't got a clue, who I am. They know nothing real about me."

She leant back on her chair, scrutinising him and he felt heat rising in his cheeks.

"Uh-huh," she got up and started collecting her things, "Look, I don't fancy you. I might be the only female in the entire building who doesn't but I just don't, okay? I stuck your food on my finger because you were hungry. You paid me back, we're cool. Don't make it uncool by running some kind of crappy teen drama scam on me. I don't want to sound like a line from a book but this," she made a sweeping gesture to indicate her face, "doesn't change if I take off my invisible glasses, let my hair grow, pluck my eyebrows and slap on a bit of make up. I don't have time for this. Besides, you're really not my type."

Her speech was slow and measured. Each word came out fully formed, the aural equivalent of having all the i-s dotted and all the t-s crossed.

Tull realised that somewhere along the lines she'd had to work hard on this and he wondered how badly deformed she'd been at birth, how many operations she'd had to endure.

She was about to leave and he needed to stall her.

He picked up the last piece of paper she hadn't gathered up yet, holding on to it while searching her eyes again.

"That's me told," he smiled earnestly then glanced at the sheet.

There were a series of roughly drawn rectangles on it with lines snaking within them, bits of song lyrics by their side and some acronyms he couldn't fathom. He narrowed his eyes, studying the hieroglyphs in front of him. A vague memory flickered up and he laughed.

"I know what this is," he exclaimed, "It's a manege. These are horse riding figures, right? This," he traced a finger along a line, "is a change of rein across the diagonal, right? I remember that. But how does the music fit in?"

She took the paper from his hand and started putting it away.

"It's a dressage-to-music routine. It's a display for a charity day at my yard. – Has your mum got a horse somewhere or something?"

Tull cocked his head and looked up at her, "Why does everyone always assume that riding is for girls? No, my mum hasn't got a horse somewhere or something. I wish."

It had come a lot more angrily than he'd intended but she smiled then, nevertheless. Still closed lipped, but it almost reached her eyes.

"You like horses?"

"Yeah," he answered curtly.

"You ride?"

He shook his head and got up.

"No. There was never any money for it. And, you know," he snorted sarcastically, "boys don't ride, right? – See you around, Liberty. And good luck with your charity day."

~~~

It was Saturday mid-morning, his mum had gone out to see the group of student counsellors she supervised once a month and Tull felt at a bit of a loss. His shift at the supermarket didn't start until 1pm and there was nothing he could think of that he wanted to watch or play or do until then.

He felt like this a lot of the time lately, like he was supposed to be doing *something else* with his life time, and his encounter the day before had amplified that feeling manifold.

There had been so much purpose in her scribbles, so much focus, so much love.

Liberty.

He sighed loudly into the emptiness of his room, went to the bathroom and ran a bath.

Half an hour later, he heard a noise downstairs through the open bathroom door.

The letter box flap opened, followed by a soft thud on the mat. Curious, he dragged himself out of the tub, wrapped a towel around his hips and went down the stairs, trailing water behind him.

On the floor in the hallway lay a brown jiffy bag. The original address, Brownleaf Stables, had been crossed out and TULL written above it in fat marker pen.

He'd just dried his hands on the towel to pick it up when he suddenly thought he could hear hooves in the distance outside.

Without a thought he opened the front door and the full force of the cold winter air hit his naked torso. He stepped out nevertheless to look up and down the road and sure enough, the big rump of a black, hairy Vanner was just disappearing around the corner. Tull had been too late to see the rider but his thumping heart had its own ideas.

He stepped back inside with chattering teeth, shut the door and picked up the parcel. He took it upstairs to his bedroom, climbed under the duvet and ripped it open.

There was a book inside.

He extracted it and a note fluttered out. He turned the paperback in his hand. On the cover was a horse's head but despite the pink lettering of the title it didn't really look like a girlie book. It looked kind of cool and well thumbed. Like a book that had been read a million times.

He picked up the letter.

Tull,

Got Amelia to tell me where you live. Hope that's ok.

Just wanted to say sorry if I came across as rude yesterday.

I haven't got much practise in talking to boys that I don't share any DNA with. Actually, make that none.

You asked why everyone always makes the assumption that boys don't ride. It's not true. Most of the best riders in the world are still men.

I don't know if you read much but I've enclosed one of my favourite books of all time for you to borrow (I'd like it back please). One of the main characters in it is a boy who rides. There are many other *books about boys and their horses, like "The Black Stallion" series and the "Flicka" trilogy but most of them were written in the 1940s. This one is set in the here and now and it is very special to me. Hope you like it.*

Liberty

Her writing was as measured and neat as her speech had been. He read the note a dozen or so times before he picked up the book again.

If he was honest, despite being a stickler for grammar and capable of beating his mum at Scrabble any day, he wasn't much of a reader but as he turned the dog-eared volume over, his eyes caught on the word 'scar-faced' among the blurb on the back.

It dawned on him then that this was more than a story to her. He crawled further under the duvet, opened it and began to read.

It was twenty to one when he realised that he was definitely going to be late for work.

~~~

The big friendly chestnut pushed its nose into Tull's cupped hands and tenderly snuffled around his palms, leaving the boy with goose bumps all over. While his outer shell was leaning nonchalantly against the stable door outside of which the horse was tied up, on the inside little Tull was excitedly jumping up and down with amazement.

He'd simply strolled in.

Just like that.

Heart in hand he'd hurried past the sign into the yard, headed for the indoor stable block adjacent to what looked like a massive barn structure and had walked through the entrance into the wide aisle that divided two long rows of stable boxes.

He had never imagined it to be this easy.

There were a fair number of people about, grooming their horses, mucking out or tacking down after their Sunday afternoon ride. As he'd arrived, one girl had just finished saddling a woolly looking bay pony and was leading it out through another door situated somewhere between the row of boxes on the right, into the main building.

He had surveyed the picture in front of him and had soon recognised the sun around which all these people-horse planets were orbiting. She was an older lady with short salt-and-pepper hair who was crouching down by the left hind leg of a large, fidgety chestnut, trying to bandage it up.

Tull had made a beeline for the horse and was now standing by its head, still unacknowledged by the human but more than appreciated by the animal, which had started licking his palms with long, sloppy drags of the tongue.

"You!" the woman looked up and narrowed her eyes at Tull, crinkling up her abundance of laughter lines, "Whatever it is you're doing at the front there, keep doing it. The oaf is finally standing still."

She returned to wrapping the leg and when she was finished got up slowly, a hand on her back.

"Ugh, I'm getting old. Thank you for your help. You might want to take the hand away now. If he likes the taste of someone, he'll go on forever. And he likes *you*."

Tull waited until the chestnut had finished testing out the spaces between his fingers with the tip of its tongue and had returned to long licks of the palm before he took the hand away. He dried it on his jeans and raised it to stroke the horse's strong neck.

"That's alright," he said, looking into the eye of the animal, "I like him, too."

"I can see that," the woman answered with laughter in her voice, "I'm Lisa Vance, I run this ship, what can I do for you?"

Tull dragged his attention away from the horse and turned to her fully.

"I'm looking for Liberty."

Suddenly the woman's demeanour changed completely. All humour drained from her eyes as she looked him up and down, unashamedly appraising his worthiness. If there had been space Tull would have taken a step back. He quickly got the feeling that he was being found entirely wanting.

"She lent me something. I've come to give it back," he added quickly to justify his temporary existence in this solar system.

The woman nodded tersely then indicated the door the bay pony had disappeared through earlier.

"She's in there. Riding."

"Thank you," Tull replied and started making towards the gap between the boxes.

"You can't go through that way," Lisa Vance sighed loudly, "But if you turn left out of the building, there is a side entrance to the spectator area."

Tull followed her directions and soon found himself inside an indoor manege, standing on the raised floor next to the sand school, leaning against the solid wooden panel that separated arena from platform. Behind him were three tiers of solid stage rises complete with rows of empty seats.

There were three riders in the school, all obviously exercising their horses to their own agenda. One was the girl on the shaggy and rather overweight pony, another was a woman who was riding a tall ribby dapple grey and then there were Liberty and the same black gypsy cob she had delivered the parcel on the day before. Or so Tull assumed. The rump looked the same. The rest of the pony was as roundly muscled as its rear and its bones thick set and heavy. Nevertheless it seemed surprisingly agile and light footed.

Presently, Liberty and the cob were cantering along the long side of the arena, with some change of movement every three strides. The long mane and feathers of the pony were flying with the motion, making it look like a wild, beautiful dance.

Indeed, the whole scene reminded him of the ballroom his mum had dragged him to on their holiday to Tenerife four years ago. Only that ballroom had been hot and sticky whereas in here it was freezing.

In front of him the three pairs of dancers commanded the floor, each pair in its own world, weaving figures and changing speed in entirely uncorrelated patterns.

Tull couldn't help wondering how on earth they didn't bump into one another but after a while he realised that there was some kind of traffic code in operation.

The woman on the grey slowed down to a walk, steered away from the outside lane, rested the reins on her horse's neck, placed a leg in front of the saddle, lifted the flap and loosened the girth underneath. The girl on the bay and Liberty were currently trotting in opposite directions of travel. They passed each other, left shoulder to left shoulder, before the girl on the bay did exactly what the grey's rider had done. Liberty turned around in the next corner, still at a trot, and rode up to the girl's side. She slowed her cob to a walk, put the reins in her left hand and extracted an earphone from her right ear. They were walking two abreast towards where Tull was standing now but Liberty still didn't appear to have noticed him.

"She's never going to lose any weight like this, Charlotte," he heard Liberty scold the girl, "You don't just ride around for twenty minutes and then give up. She needs more exercise. You need to get her heart rate going. If she looks like this now, in the middle of winter, what do you think she's going to look like in spring? She'll end up with laminitis again."

The girl shrugged, "I'm cold, Lips. I want to go home."

They'd come level with Tull now and the boy's heart was beating in his throat. They rode past him and it promptly sank to the bottom of his stomach.

"Well, if you ride her properly, it'll soon warm you up. Don't just let her carry you, *ride* her," Liberty continued and shook her head in obvious dismay, reining her own pony to a halt. She made it go backwards five neat steps then stopped next to Tull, patting the neck of the black.

"Good boy," she praised the pony before cocking her head to look at Tull.

Evidently, it was frown time again.

Before she could say anything, Tull pulled the paperback out of his bag and laid it on top of the partition.

"I've come to return this," he explained.

"Oh," beyond the frown her face momentarily seemed to fall but the inscrutable mask quickly took over, "You didn't want to read it then?"

"What? No. I've read it. I loved it. It is singlehandedly responsible for me getting about four hours sleep in the last twenty-four hours. I couldn't put it down. And I don't normally read. It's a really cool book, Liberty, thank you," feeling extremely self-conscious all of a sudden in the beam of her sparkling eyes, he diverted his attention to the pony who was still standing good as gold, "He's a Vanner, isn't he?"

She leant onto her pony's neck and smiled at him, a proper big smile that showed the teeth, "That's what the Americans usually call them but yes, he is. We usually say Irish Cob."

"Or Gypsy Cob?"

"Or Gypsy Cob," she agreed, catching his flitting eyes again, "I need to warm him down now but if you've got time, do you want me to show you around the yard afterwards?"

~~~

It was still pitch black when Tull left his house the next morning and he pondered for a while when he'd last risen so early out of his own free will. He put the hood of his kagool up to protect his head from the constant cold drizzle and wished he'd chosen a thicker jacket.

As he walked briskly towards his destination, he tried to remember all the horses' names she'd introduced him to the day before as well as all the other bits and pieces of information she'd strewn like breadcrumbs along their way around the yard. Their round had consisted of almost three hours in the end, during which she had effortlessly woven him into her duties.

'Hold this', 'Muck out that', 'Here, this is how you do this,' had constituted most of their conversation. And Tull had loved every minute of it. He'd got to help her bring in horses from the field, brush and feed them, refill hay nets and put night rugs on.

At times he'd asked himself whether he was more of a hindrance than a help but if he had been then Liberty had not let on. On the contrary, she had been a patient, kind tutor, always cool and reserved but also encouraging even when he'd got stuff wrong.

The only thing marring the experience had been Lisa Vance's obvious antipathy. The owner of Brownleaf Stables couldn't have made it any clearer that she didn't like him hanging around but when he'd mentioned it to Liberty on the way home she'd shrugged it off.

"Hang around and she'll come around," she had said during their goodbyes on her doorstep, "We could really do with an extra pair of hands right now. Especially with the charity day coming up. She'd adore you already if you had an eye missing or a limp or really bad acne. You're just too pretty is your problem. If you can show her you're a grafter, she'll start seeing the ugly inside and then you'll be fine."

It was by far one of the weirdest things anyone had ever said to him but he'd heard the invitation wrapped inside it.

Although standing outside her house now, at stupid o'clock in the morning waiting for her to emerge he began doubting whether she'd meant it. Liberty's face when she stepped out of the door and spotted him didn't reassure him either. She stopped in front of him, silently did up the long oil skin coat she was wearing and then looked into his eyes incredulously.

"What on earth are you doing here?"

Tull shrugged and mustered his widest smile.

"You said you needed help and that you start at half past five. I figured we'd walk together."

She kept staring at him as if frozen in time and Tull felt reminded of when she'd dressed him down in the dinner hall. He hoped she wasn't going to repeat the performance and just leave him standing here.

Finally she shook her head.

"I thought maybe you might want to come for a couple of hours in the afternoon some days, like yesterday. Help out a bit. I didn't realise you were going to apply for *my* job."

"I'm not. I just thought...I wasn't expecting to get paid or anything...I just...oh man...do you want me to go away?" he stuttered feeling like a complete fool.

Suddenly she laughed and took his hand.

"Don't be silly. You are here now," she started walking, dragging him along, "and you'll make a great slave. Because as for payment? There isn't any. After a couple of months Lisa might offer you some free lessons. Might. If you're reliable. After a couple of years of servitude and if she thinks your riding is up to it she might offer you the permanent loan of a horse with free livery and feed in return for your continued devotion. Might. If you are lucky. You'll still have to find the money for the farrier and the vet yourself though," she sighed deeply and let go of his hand.

Just in time, he thought with a twinge, for the original gesture not to become awkward or meaningful.

"Which can be really tough when there isn't enough food in the cupboard at home," she added after a pause.

Tull could only imagine.

Compared to Liberty's family Tull and his mum were positively rich. The fact that he'd compared his own momentary hunger the day they had met to any she had experienced in her life made his ears burn when he thought about it now.

It was amazing how much he'd already known about the girl who was presently walking silently by his side through the increasingly dense rain without ever realising.

As soon as they had arrived outside the shabby looking extended bungalow she lived in the day before, a whole number of jigsaw pieces had fallen into place.

One of her brothers had been in the junior football team he'd helped to coach the previous summer. The trainer had dropped both of them off once, little Jacob first, and Tull had remembered the house. Another of her brothers worked at the same supermarket. It was a large store and Tull had barely ever spoken to the guy but the other one had congratulated him on the team winning a match once. And on it went. Little nuggets of information from here, there and everywhere had tumbled into his consciousness overnight to form at least the ghost of a picture.

As far as Tull knew there were eight kids in their household altogether, cramped into one of the largest social housing properties around. They were collectively known as The Ellis Boys and Tull had always been under the impression that they were indeed all boys. He would never have associated her with them. Facial reconstruction, calluses and grubby finger nails aside she had a regal air about her with her straight posture and her confident walk that set her entirely apart from those of her siblings that he had met. There was also the fact that he could not recall ever having seen her around before that day in the school canteen despite living on opposite ends of the same estate. He on the private and she on the council side. But having listened to her gruelling daily schedule the previous afternoon he'd realised there was no real mystery there.

She got up at quarter to five every morning to be at the yard an hour later then helped until half past seven, before leaving to go home and change for school. After school she went directly back to Brownleaf until late evening, 'then home, food, homework, bed' she had added cheerfully. On weekends she spent all day at the yard other than on Sundays when she went from the morning shift there to tutoring Maths and English to the son of one of the liveries because in spite of her endless work load, Liberty was rather good at school.

They had reached the edge of the estate where the pavements ended and the country lanes began. Before they started walking single file along the grass verge Liberty stopped for a moment, took a head torch out of her coat pocket and put it on.

Soon after, they turned onto the farm track that led up to the yard, the beam from her forehead illuminating a narrow path in front of them. To the left lay the total black of a ploughed field that had carried sweet corn in the summer, much to Tull's delight. To the right the Brownleaf paddocks began, the grass giving them a slightly lighter shade of darkness. Liberty turned her head to shine the light onto a cluster of five ponies huddling around a large shelter. Tull knew this lot well, had fed them many a handful of grass over the summer when on one of his corn on the cob reconnaissance missions. There were four almost identical looking duns whose withers came to his shoulder and his personal friend, a little grey Shetland who was always the first to gallop to the fence. Liberty took a key out of her pocket and opened the bicycle chain that secured the gate.

"Right, first we get this lot to the yard. They're getting their feet done later today, so they'll go in till then. Do you think you can handle leading two at a time? If I show you how? It's okay to say if you don't think you can manage. I can't think of anyone else I'd ask on their second day around horses ever but you seemed quite capable yesterday and it would save an awful lot of time."

"It's fine," he reassured her, the unexpected compliment showering him in confidence and silly pride. As he followed her into the paddock and to the shelter, he stepped in a puddle and mud squelched into his already soaked trainers, dousing his feet in ice-cold water but he bit his tongue. He didn't want her to think him a limp biscuit after all.

"Wait here a minute," she instructed, parking him amidst the ponies.

She disappeared to the back of the shelter, taking the light with her.

Five soft noses pushed towards him in the dark, sniffing and breathing warm air over his freezing hands. He petted them softly while he listened to Liberty rummaging around to the rhythm of the rain drumming a steady beat onto the corrugated iron roof above them. Despite the cold and wet, the darkness and the absurdity of the hour, despite the smell of mud, damp horse, ammonia and manure Tull suddenly felt a warm glow spread through his core.

Belonging.

This was where he'd belonged all along.

Liberty pushed her way back through the ponies holding a maglite and a bunch of headcollars. She took the head torch off and gave it to Tull.

"Here, you take this. I can lead and hold a torch at the same time. You're not qualified for that yet. You'll have these two," she pointed at two of the duns, "Toffee and Butterscotch. They are as good as gold. I'll put the headcollars on, show you how to lead them and then I'll take the other two and you follow me out."

"What about this little guy?" Tull asked, scratching his favourite around the withers while the pony sniffed the boy's knees. The Shetland was the only one of the five that didn't wear a rug and as Tull stroked along his spine a mess of wet and muddy hair stuck to his fingers.

"Titch? He doesn't need leading. If we take the others out, he'll follow. Ready?"

"Ready."

~~~

It took almost three weeks for Lisa Vance to finally warm to him a little.

After seven days, when he'd turned up alongside Liberty every morning she'd finally stopped scowling at him. After a fortnight she had given him her first direct order. On the morning of the twentieth day, after Liberty and he had mucked out the stables, turned out who needed to be turned out and brought in who needed to be brought in, she offered him a cup of tea.

Lisa stepped out of the little office that was situated at the back of the stable block carrying a small tray with three steaming mugs and approached the last box that was being readied for the day.

Inside the box Liberty had just opened a bale of straw and was spreading it out, while Tull was grooming little Titch in the aisle. The Shetland kept ripping at a second bale by the stable door and Tull gently poked the fat belly under the thick wool of the gelding's winter coat.

"Piglet," he cooed lovingly.

Tull had yet to be invited to sit on a horse at Brownleaf Stables but in the meantime he had adopted the smallest pony on the yard as his to care for. Nobody had given him permission or asked him to do so but he'd figured out quickly that the Shetland was regarded as somewhat pointless and surplus to requirement in a yard where the youngest regular rider was already twelve years old. Though fed and looked after with the rest of them Titch didn't have anyone else that paid him special attention, so Tull had quietly begun taking him out to groom whenever there wasn't another job to do or when Liberty was training with Oliver, her cob. Sometimes they would walk along when Liberty took Gingerbread Man, Lisa's old arthritic chestnut, which had made Tull feel so welcome on his first visit, on gentle hacks out. Occasionally little girls would come to ride Titch on the lead rein – nieces, cousins or little sisters of other riders at Brownleaf - and Tull had quickly become the person of choice for the other end of the rope.

Lisa arrived with the tray on the opposite side of the Shetland and put it down on the bale. She handed the boy a mug.

"Thank you."

"You're welcome. - Liberty?" she shouted over her shoulder, "Your tea's here. Come out for a second, I want to talk to you both about the charity day."

Lisa turned back to Tull who was warming his hands on the thick china and blowing on his tea. She took a swig of her own brew, examining him over the rim of her mug almost as if for the first time.

"How are you finding the early mornings?" she asked evenly.

"Early," he answered with a small smile then took a breath, "Easy when I'm here, difficult when I'm at school."

Lisa nodded.

"You get used to it after about twenty years. What do your folks make of you spending all your time here?"

Tull shrugged, "My mum believes in self-actualisation, I'm self-actualising."

There was the tiniest jerk of surprise in Lisa's neck and she cocked her head slightly, examining him more closely.

Tull dropped his eyes and ruffled the Shetland's forehead. As soon as he'd stopped brushing, Titch had let off the bale and started nuzzling the boy's knees nudging him to carry on.

"Can I ask you a question?" Tull enquired softly, looking back up.

"I don't know," Lisa answered with a glint in her eye, "but you can try."

Tull dared to grin, "Okay, let me rephrase that, *may* I ask you a question?"

"You may."

"Whose is he?"

Lisa looked pointedly from boy to Shetland and back from Shetland to boy, "Yours at the moment."

"No, really," Tull was getting frustrated. He didn't want to spar, he just wanted to know but at the same time he didn't want to offend the woman now that she'd finally acknowledged his presence, "Who does he belong to?"

"According to his passport he is mine but, really, he is nobody's anymore," she studied the frown on Tull's face and smiled sadly, "He belonged to a little boy. A little boy called Joseph who died from leukaemia seven years ago. He made me promise I would look after Titch until he dies, too," she gulped down a mouthful of tea, "Thing is, he's seventeen now, those little buggers can make it to forty, I'm fifty-two in January, chances are he's going to outlive me."

"Don't say that," sniggered Liberty who'd come out, taken her mug and sat down on the bale stretching out her long legs, "With good veterinary care and some decent winter rugs we'll get you right into your eighties."

Lisa turned to the girl with a smile so big that it crinkled up her eyes until they disappeared into their sockets and suddenly Tull realised that there was much more to these two than the master-minion bond Liberty often joked about. The older woman had given him such a wide berth until now that he hadn't seen them interact before. Now he could see that there was true affection here, way beyond a connection forged by their shared love of horses. He watched Liberty sip her tea and look from Lisa to him and back.

"Right," the girl nodded, "so what did you want to talk to us about? I've got an appointment with a shower and a stack of pancakes provided my brothers haven't worked out where my secret stash is yet."

It was long after Lisa had finished running through the list of things they still needed to organise, had already made her way back to the office and shut the door behind her when Liberty nudged Tull and grinned at him.

"Well done, you."

"So you reckon she can see the ugly inside yet?"

The girl regarded him with serious, heavy eyes that set his whole being alight. Each cell in his body seemed to shudder separately under her scrutiny.

"Is there any?" she asked quietly after a moment and held his gaze.

If she had been any other girl he would have tried to kiss her then, would have finally given it a shot to find out what those ragged edged lips tasted like.

But she wasn't any other girl.

She was Liberty, holding the door open to where he belonged.

~~~

They dropped Titch off in his field and carried on walking unhurriedly. It was Saturday and with no school to go to they had lingered over their chores longer than on weekdays. As they made their way to the end of the farm track the sun rose on what promised to become a glorious December day. A couple of cars were turning onto the track, horse owners coming for an early hack. The first car crawled by, careful to avoid the potholes. The second was packed to the brim with teenage girls, chauffeured by a harassed looking woman, less mindful of the road conditions.

She swerved to avoid the walking pair and Tull recognised the group. The woman at the wheel and three of the girls, her daughters, had their own horse and came every day, the other girl was a part-time loaner who only ever appeared at the weekends. They waved and Tull waved back. He could see them turn to one another, giggling.

"What's it like?" Liberty asked when they had passed by.

"What is what like?

"Being that attractive. Having girls swoon over you wherever you go."

He couldn't pretend that he didn't know what she was talking about. He'd always been the object of a fair number of females' desire at school but at Brownleaf, by the nature of the beast a nest crawling with teenage girls where the only other male was a retired mounted police officer, it had reached almost epic proportions. Much as Tull loved the early morning shift alongside Liberty alone, he often dreaded coming back in the afternoon when the yard was heaving. Especially when she was not by his side, riding out or off with Lisa, he generally tried to avoid the stable block and spent time in the field with Titch and the duns instead.

"Objectifying," he replied wryly and glanced at her sideways in time to see a small smile curl around her mouth.

They had rounded the corner to the country lane and he slipped in behind her on the verge. As he watched her straight back, her elegant legs taking their measured strides he suddenly felt distinctly honoured to be walking behind this girl and also incredibly grateful for what she'd done for him so far.

"Liberty?" he shouted at her over the noise of the traffic zooming past.

"Yes?" she shouted into the air above her.

"Those pancakes, do they come in a packet?"

"Afraid so."

He swallowed and told his heart to shut up for a second.

"How would you like me to make you some real ones?"

She stopped abruptly and turned on her heels to face him.

He'd thought he'd learned the whole dictionary of Liberty frowns over the last three weeks but this was a new one still. It came with eyes narrowed to slits and a half raised eyebrow.

He held his breath.

"Tempting," she finally replied, "But at what price?"

"Eternal gratitude?"

"Too expensive."

He stepped up to her close enough so they didn't have to raise their voices any longer.

"No, mine," he said quietly, "They are more than paid for, Liberty. I just want to thank you, that's all."

She tilted her head to look up into his eyes, "You're still not my type, you know."

It hurt but he managed to mask it with a grin, "That's okay, as long my pancakes are."

She stepped aside, "Lead on, McDuff."

~~~

"They were fantastic. You are a great chef. I'm stuffed," Liberty pushed the plate away and crossed her arms on the table, "Not just a pretty face, are ya?"

"They are just pancakes. You want to come for dinner and try my ratatouille some time."

She leant forward, examining him, "Dinner? Are you *still* trying to get into my pants?"

"Liberty Ellis!" he exclaimed trying to hide the blood rushing to his face by getting up and collecting their dishes.

"Sorry. Seven brothers, you know. - You're blushing," she stated with an amused twitch of the nose, "You know, that was one of the first things I noticed about you. You're a blusher. It's quite sweet."

"Well," he mumbled looking down, "you're not making it any better right now."

He quickly made for the safe haven of the kitchen and took a breather before he returned to the living room.

This was much harder than he'd thought.

As long as they were at the yard or walking to or from it things had a pre-prescribed rhythm and at school nothing had really changed. Liberty had no interest in sitting with his friends, neither had Tull any longer if he was honest but the unwritten rules of separation still applied. He sat with his group and she sat on her own, working. In one way or another she was always busy and this was the first time he was with her without a blueprint to follow.

When he came back to the table she had half turned in her chair, looking around the room with interest.

"So, when did you learn to cook like that?" she asked, still surveying the surroundings.

He shrugged and sat back down.

"It's just my mum and me, she often works till late, so I picked up a cook book a couple of years ago and started. I like it. It's relaxing."

She turned back to him and smiled.

"I can't even imagine a house with only two people in it. What does your mum do?"

"She's a counsellor."

"She gives people advice on their problems?"

"No. That's not how it works. She's more like a listener. She listens while you work out your own solutions. But it's like, *proper* listening. What does yours do?"

"My mum? No idea. She's not around anymore. Probably collects dolls. She scarpered after Jacob was born. You know Jake, right? You coached him last summer. Strange woman, my mother. I saw a programme on women who are addicted to being pregnant once and I think that was her problem. You would have thought she'd had enough when baby number five came out with a gaping hole in the face but no, she carried on getting impregnated. After Jake though, her uterus pretty much fell out and she couldn't have any more. Soon as she weaned him, she just packed up and left."

"What about your dad? What does he do?"

It wasn't the question he had really wanted to ask but here was that side of her again that he feared, the jaded beyond her years one that said 'if you put a foot wrong you'll just become part of my cynicism'.

"Are you kidding? With eight kids to look after on his own? He's professionally unemployed. He used to be a roofer. – Go on, ask me what you really want to ask me."

"This," he touched his own mouth, "did it hurt?"

"When I was born? No idea. The first operation? Probably. I don't know. I was seven months old, I can't remember. The second one was excruciating though. I was nine. What hurt more though was that people always assumed I was stupid because I couldn't speak properly. Even the silly SENCO woman at my primary didn't get it. Special educational needs coordinator, my foot. She had special needs herself. One of them being that she couldn't have organised a piss up in a brewery, to quote my dad. There is me, already reading and writing at a level way above my year and everybody still thinks I'm an idiot and have behavioural problems. Of course I had behavioural problems. I was frustrated because I couldn't make anyone understand and angry because nobody understood. There are still plenty of people who think I'm slow because I speak slowly. But I didn't get a proper speech therapist until we moved here and Lisa and Christine got a friend of theirs to see me twice a week."

"Who is Christine?" Tull asked quietly, not wanting to interrupt her flow.

She caught him out though, smiling, "Works this listening business, doesn't it? – Christine was Lisa's girlfriend. She was the qualified instructor out of the two. Although Lisa is better in my opinion but I can hardly remember Christine teaching to be fair. When I arrived she already didn't want to be there anymore. They split up a couple of months after I turned up. Joseph had already been dead a year but Lisa says that's what killed the relationship. Some parents grow closer when they lose their children, others grow apart. They grew apart."

Tull gulped, "Titch is Lisa's dead son's pony?"

Liberty nodded.

"Technically, Christine's dead son's but yeah, that pretty much sums it up," she pushed the chair away from the table and got up, "I've got to go. I've got a list of things to buy in town before I go back to the yard later."

As Tull silently accompanied her to the door, a possibility occurred to him that he hadn't even considered before.

"Liberty?"

"Yep?" she replied, pulling her boots on.

"Are you…" he didn't know how to ask without failing miserably in crossing the minefield of insinuation that spread out in front of him, so he stopped himself.

"Am I what?" Liberty straightened up before opening the door, "Lisa's underage teenage gay lover?" she enquired with derisive laughter in the back of her throat, "No. She is my boss and my mentor and the woman who gave me speech and whose name is on my pony's passport. And a friend. She is also 37 years older than me. That would be just wrong. And illegal. Let's not forget illegal. And despicable. And just…yikes."

For a moment Tull stood and stared in wonder at the mines exploding without him even touching one fuse then he sighed.

"That wasn't what I was going to ask."

The girl laughed, a teasing sound.

"I know," she turned to him fully, took his hand and kissed the back of it lightly, "Thank you for breakfast," she held his hand a moment longer smiling broadly up at him, "And no, I'm not gay as far as I know. I – just - don't - fancy - *you*."

She let go, punched him lightly on the shoulder and left.

~~~

As the charity day approached Tull slowly began feeling like an actual part of Brownleaf. Whereas before he had known hardly anyone by name with the exception of Liberty, Lisa and Amelia's mother, it was like he had suddenly been put on a crash course in putting names to faces to horses.

Everyone at the yard was chipping in during the preparations and Tull seemed to be everybody's favourite boy Friday. One day he was helping Richard, the retired police officer who owned a big bay Warmblood called Gulliver, reinforce the wheelchair access ramp that led to the viewing platform in the indoor school and dismantle the rows of seats until only the bare wooden stage rises were left. The next was spent collecting foldaway tables from the church hall down the road to create a banqueting table on the highest rise. The one after he accompanied Lisa in the horsebox to pick up a number of patio heaters from a bar owner called Claire who he had seen riding her spirited dapple-grey Thoroughbred Callisto in the school the day he'd first come to the yard. The actual day before the event, while everyone else was polishing horses and sorting out the last bits at the stables, he found himself working alongside a woman by the name of Martina and her three daughters in the kitchen of his dreams, helping prepare food for the big day. Between them they owned Sheila, a much spoiled, very placid palomino Arab who was ridden Western style.

After they had prepped and cling-filmed the last container, Martina drove them all back to the yard for a final gathering of volunteers.

Bales of straw had been put out to line the aisle for people to sit on and soon everyone was perched looking expectantly at the office door, waiting for Lisa and Liberty to emerge with last instructions. They came out side by side and Tull forgot to breathe for a minute.

Liberty was wearing a costume made of thigh high soft brown leather boots, beige breeches and a multicoloured velvet waistcoat hung with little bells over a golden silk shirt. To complete the outfit she had knotted a bright red shawl around her waist, making her look somewhere between stolen gypsy princess and fair maiden pirate. She caught his eye and smiled, sending a shiver of longing down his spine.

"Right," Lisa commanded the collected attention, "I have the final list of names now. We have eight coming tomorrow. All between twelve and sixteen except one little one who's just turned seven. The oldest one has an oxygen tank, so she is for you and Gulliver, Richard. One is in a wheelchair and is apparently very weak so I reckon she is best off in a Western saddle. So that'll obviously be Sheila's job, Martina. Then there is one who is pretty much blind and Liberty and I figure she'll get the most out of going bareback, so that's one for Oliver. There are four who are still relatively fit, so that'll be Toffee's, Peanut's, Butterscotch's and Caramel's lot. You lot can sort out amongst yourselves who leads which pony."

She looked at Martina's daughters and a fourth girl called India who part-loaned Peanut out of the foursome of duns that formed the rest of Titch's little herd. Lisa paused, exchanged a look with Liberty who nodded sharply and then took a deep breath before addressing Tull.

"Which brings me to you. Do you think you could lead Titch with the little one on board?"

Tull was gaping at her and Lisa frowned. Suddenly realisation spread across her face.

"Has anyone actually bothered to explain to you what tomorrow is about?"

He silently shook his head.

~~~

They arrived by minibus the next morning.

A motley crew of shaven heads and puffy, pale faces; aliens from another planet whose mere existence made one's own woes pale into insignificance.

Tull stared as Lisa went to meet and greet them, painfully ashamed of how he saw them yet helpless in the face of his instinctive detachment.

Right at the end, after all and sundry had already been unloaded a young, pretty, dark-haired woman descended the steps of the bus carrying a little girl in a bobble hat on her hip. The little girl looked around the yard, eyes wide with excitement. She spotted Tull by the entrance to the stable block and waved. Tull swallowed the lump in his throat, forced a smile and waved back.

Distracted by the woman who was carrying her, the girl looked away and he let his hand sink to his side. A calloused, slender palm slipped inside it and deft, reassuring fingers weaved themselves through his. He felt their owner rise onto tip-toes next to him, followed by her warm breath flowing over his cold cheek.

"Chin up," Liberty's voice whispered in his ear, "Just don't bawl, okay? I promise you by the end of the day you'll think you've never had more fun in your life."

She lowered herself back onto her heels and detangled her hand from his. Bereft of the protection of intimacy, he suddenly felt the icy coldness of the air around them seep into his bones.

"I'll be alright," he stated shivering, "I just don't get why we are not doing this in the summer, when it's warm."

"We do," Liberty responded already half turned away to go and find her charge, "but they're only looked after by the charity for the last few months, so we do two a year. One in June, one in December. The ones who came in the summer are not around anymore and these guys won't be around by next summer. That's how it is. – Go say hello to her, her name is Jessica."

Halfway through the day, caught up in a feverish discussion about the best horse colours and what names went well with them, Liberty's words suddenly came back to him.

She'd been right. He couldn't remember ever having had this much fun.

When he'd gone to meet her, Jessica had seamlessly moved from her perch on her mum's hip over to him and when not cuddling or grooming Titch now clung to Tull like a monkey, asking question after question. Her dark eyes shone brightly under her bobble hat as they drank in every detail of her surroundings and her spindly arms gave his neck happy little squeezes with each answer he gave. Most of the time Tull simply forgot that she wasn't just a normal little girl excited to be around ponies.

But then there were moments of stark contrast.

When she had to call on her mum to have her nappy changed, embarrassedly telling him that *really* she'd been out of nappies by one-and-a-half or when she had to swap the bobble hat for a riding helmet and made him stroke the few remaining tufts of black hair on her brittle skinned scalp.

They were standing in the tack room, Jessica by his feet. Everyone was there, trying hats out on riders and he found Liberty's eyes, taking strength from the sharp nod she gave him.

The little girl tugged at his jumper.

"You like her," she stated with a knowing smile.

Tull nodded slowly as he clicked the clasp of the chin strap in place, "Yes I do."

Jessica examined Liberty intently for a few moments.

"She isn't pretty."

Tull smiled down at her before he picked her up to set her back on his hip.

"Ah, this is where you are wrong. To me, she is the prettiest girl in the universe."

He saw Jessica's face fall and put a finger to the tip of her nose.

"In the over seven category only, of course," he winked at her, "It's a good thing she doesn't have to compete against you or I wouldn't know which one of you to pick."

"You really think I'm pretty?" the little girl asked quietly.

He looked into her eyes, so dark they seemed to go on forever and gave her his best smile.

"Very."

It earned him a huge hug, her riding hat pushing painfully into his temple as she squeezed him hard. He hugged her back gingerly, feeling her fragile body beneath his fingers and swallowed back the tears that suddenly wanted to come so badly.

He opened his eyes over her shoulder and looked at Liberty who was just leading Eileen, the blind girl, past.

"I heard that," Liberty said loudly and grinned at him, "Competition, huh? I'm not sure I like it."

He knew it was only meant to be a joke, a light-heartedly thrown lifebelt of flirtatiousness, to stop him from going to pieces, but the glance that came with it made his stomach lurch nevertheless.

"Come on, people," Liberty continued as she passed through the door, "Let's ride!"

~~~

And so they rode.

To begin with they took to the indoor school to get everyone on. Jessica was the first to mount and sat atop Titch, hugging the pony from above while watching the others clamber onto their horses. Her mum waved from the sideline, clutching the bobble hat to her chest and Jessica waved back before rolling her face over Titch's neck to look at Tull again.

"I hope mummy has another baby. So she has someone to cuddle. Cuddling is the best," she gave the pony another squeeze then sat up, indicating Gulliver and the girl who'd come with a little portable oxygen tank, "How come his saddle has a thingy for Brooke's air?"

Tull watched Richard and Lisa sort out the rider in question.

"It's not really for that. Richard and Gulliver go on long rides around England to map out bridle routes and he takes a tent and other stuff. That's what those saddle bags are normally for."

Jessica's eyes became even larger, "He goes camping with his horse? I want to do that. That sounds fun. I love camping," she paused and for the first time that day sadness crept into her voice, "We used to go all the time."

Before Tull could find any words to reply, all riders were settled on their animals, all leaders in position and they started walking. Jessica wobbled a little, giggled and then found the rhythm of the pony as they slipped in behind the rest of the horses.

Lisa was walking along the line of riders, correcting people's positions, checking for comfort and giving kind words. Finally she came to the trio at the rear.

"You sit very nicely Jessica," a big smile crinkled up Lisa's face, "Now be careful for your legs not to ride up otherwise you fall off. Keep them nice and long. Are you comfy?"

Jessica nodded happily and Lisa moved off to the centre of the school. She looked on silently as the troupe finished a round.

"Right," she bellowed, "if anyone's not liking it, tell me now because if you're all good, it's time to go out into the woods."

Nobody made a sound and Lisa opened the side door to the outside world. Moments later the procession left the school.

The day on the other side was cold, dry and bluish grey. They turned out of the yard and Tull watched each team round the corner. The breath of the horses appeared in little white clouds in front of their nostrils as they blew out their noses one by one, making Gulliver with all his trappings and Brooke with the tubes running to her nose look like a machination from the steam era.

Behind them Liberty, Oliver and the blind girl seemed almost bare in comparison without a saddle, the cob wearing just a roller with a hoop for the girl to steady herself on.

Next in line were Martina, Sheila and the most skeletal of the gang, a girl called Victoria who was holding on to the horn of the mare's Western saddle with both hands.

Following in their footsteps were the four duns and their riders who from a distance looked like any group of teens enjoying their first time on a horse. Their ponies were more bunched together than the three horses at the front and the girls on top chatted away amongst themselves and with their leaders.

He wondered for a moment how Jessica, Titch and he would look to an observer.

His question was answered almost immediately by Lisa. She was walking behind the company on foot alongside one of the charity's nurses, a big bear-like man who'd introduced himself as Brian.

"The three of you are just the cutest. - Go on make him trot up to the others. You're getting left behind. Hold on tight, Jessica," Lisa ordered.

Tull made the girl grip the balancing strap on Titch's saddle before he clicked his tongue. They jogged up to Butterscotch's big behind. Titch's little legs were going rapidly like sewing machine needles and Jessica laughed in rhythm with the vibrations, a little gargling sound of pure, silly joy.

"Again!" she exclaimed when they had closed up and gone back to a walk.

Tull figured there was no harm in walking just a little slowly so that one could trot up a few more times.

~~~

The ride lasted almost an hour. Across a barren but beautiful winter landscape of fallow fields in perpetual twilight they made their way into the forest and past a little ancient chapel, famous for once having starred in a Hollywood movie.

Halfway they had to stop by the roadside and call a taxi for Victoria who couldn't hold on any longer. She sank off Sheila's saddle into Brian's arms and was carried away tenderly like a bride across the threshold. Tull caught a glimpse of her as she peeked over her helper's shoulder to take a last look at the horses, exhausted contentedness illuminating her sunken features.

She wasn't at the yard when they got back. A flower had been put in her place at the banqueting table.

~~~

Having put all the horses save Oliver away, the group of chilly and tired but exulted riders proceeded to the viewing platform in the indoor arena where the table had been laid with nibbles and the patio heaters were waiting to lull them into sleepy warmth. Jessica had moved back onto Tull's hip as soon as Titch had been left in a stable and was talking excitedly to her mum who was walking up the ramp next to them.

Once all guests were seated to face the arena and hot drinks had been served, Lisa made a sign to

Richard who was standing by the stable block entrance.

A second later Liberty rode in, a symphony of gypsy bells and colours.

She trotted Oliver down the centre line, halted in the middle of the arena, bowed to her audience and then the music started.

Jessica tugged at Tull's sleeve from her seat.

"Take me there," she pleaded, pointing down to where Tull had first stood to watch Liberty all those weeks ago. He hoisted her back onto his hip and they went down the stage rises to lean against the partition.

In the arena Oliver and Liberty were dancing to the music, a pair in perfect harmony that looked like one creature. They drew disciplined figures across the sand at first then began building towards a wild crescendo to the ancient tune coming from the PA that made your heart beat faster. They galloped the final round, all boundless power. The music changed, becoming quiet and more restrained and so did pony and rider. Liberty collected the cob into a canter and then into an ever slowing trot before turning down the centre line to stop dead centre on a penny in time with the music.

They took their bow.

"That looks such fun," Jessica clapped her hands. Behind them the rest of the audience, too, was applauding loudly and Liberty beamed up at them, while patting Oliver happily on the neck.

Slightly out of breath, her face a little blushed and for once devoid of all scepticism, she was the most stunning sight Tull had ever seen.

Liberty let the pony walk towards Jessica and him on a long rein and smiled at the little girl when she arrived in front of them.

"You enjoyed that?"

"I want to go fast like that. Can I? Can I, please?"

"It takes a long time to learn to ride like that," Liberty answered truthfully.

Disappointment washed over the little girl's face.

"I thought so," she sighed.

"But," Liberty added, "You could help me warm him down and sit on him while he walks around. Would you like that?"

Jessica nodded enthusiastically.

"In that case you two need to go to the tack room and get your hat again then come around into the school. I'll have a word with your mummy in the meantime."

As they walked back from the tack room through the stable block, filled to the brim with horses munching contentedly on their hay, Tull could sense the energy on his hip flag.

"Hey," he enquired softly, "Are you tired?"

"A little," Jessica yawned then abruptly sat up straighter, "But I'm not too tired to ride."

Tull laughed, "Yeah, I figured."

"Tull?" Jessica leant back on his hip and scrunched up her face, "Which one do *you* ride?"

He stopped for a second, "None."

"Why?"

He shrugged, "I haven't got any money for lessons."

"That is so unfair!" she exclaimed indignantly, "Everybody should be allowed to ride. It should be free!"

He drew her back against his body and started walking again, facing away from her so she couldn't see his eyes.

This little girl who had been dealt the most unfair card of all getting upset on his behalf was threatening to tip him over the edge and this time Liberty was not there to throw him a lifeline. He hurried towards the arena in big steps, suppressing his emotions harder with each stride.

When they entered the sand school Liberty was sitting astride Oliver bareback. His saddle had been taken off and slung over the side panel, where Jessica's mum was now standing. Worry and excitement mixed on her face.

Liberty rode towards them, mischievousness playing around her lips.

"Right. You're back. Are you feeling strong?" she addressed Jessica, "Then hop on behind me and hold on really tight. Tull? If you would do us the honours, sling her up."

Tull heaved the little girl onto Oliver's broad back and once she was settled wiped his eyes with the back of his hand.

"You have fun," he snivelled.

Liberty arched her eyebrows, "Oh, she will."

He should have known.

The differences between Liberty Ellis and other girls were not skin deep. They went all the way through to the core. Dashing and daring, brave and brash she was the only girl in the world he could think of who would take a dying child behind her on her pony and give it the time of its life. For there was very little warming down a horse at walk involved in what happened next.

As soon as Jessica's arms were securely fastened around her waist and the little girl had found Oliver's rhythm Liberty picked up the reins and off they went. Not at a full gallop but in a beautiful, measured canter still fast enough for Jessica to whoop with joy.

The sound rang through the arena like a battle cry of bliss.

~~~

Jessica couldn't eat the food they had prepared. She sat on Tull's lap during the meal, slurping a kind of grey looking pureed mass through a straw, talking a dime a dozen, high on adrenaline until exhaustion finally pounced from behind and she began nodding off against his shoulder.

By the time Liberty arrived at the table having put Oliver away in his stable at last, the little girl was fast asleep in his arms and Tull's limbs were rapidly going the same way. Jessica's mum who was sitting to his right was just reaching across to stroke her daughter's face when Liberty quietly pulled out the chair to his left and sat herself down. Jessica's mother looked at both of them with gratitude and sadness.

"Thank you. I couldn't have asked for better people to look after her today. You've both been absolutely wonderful. You know," her eyes singled out Tull for a moment, "she's always wanted a big brother. When she was younger she had an imaginary one, I'm glad she got to have a real one for the day," she swallowed hard and looked across at Liberty, "And you. I'll never forget what you did for her today, for us, for me. I'll remember that sound she made for the rest of my life."

Liberty clenched her teeth, nodded sharply and forced a smile.

"We aim to please," she turned to the table, "Is there any food left? I'm famished."

~~~

Dusk fell and it was time for the visitors to leave.

Tull gently woke Jessica and took her to say goodbye to Titch before carrying her onto the bus. She gave him a last hug then sleepily settled into the window seat next to her mum. He left the vehicle and stood in the yard with the other helpers, Liberty by his side, waving. His last glimpse of Jessica was her little pale palm against the pane as the minibus pulled away.

Those left behind silently began tidying up and putting the yard back to its normal state.

Titch and the duns were taken back to their paddock, while those who had lent them their stables for the day had to be brought back in, brushed down and made ready for the night.

Gingerbread Man who'd been boxed all day needed to stretch his arthritic legs in the arena before the worst of them had to be rubbed and dressed for the night. Normally this was Lisa's or Liberty's job but tonight Lisa, subdued and tired like the rest of them, handed Tull the headcollar with a few words of instruction and then retreated to her office.

Tull haltered the big, lanky chestnut and took him into the school.

There was something companionable about the friendly gelding that flowed right along the rope into Tull's arm. As he lurched alongside the boy on a slack lead, nose on the ground, sniffing out the trails the other horses had left during the day Tull slowly felt the tears he had been swallowing all day turn into an all encompassing sadness.

His hip felt empty and his heart heavy.

Gingerbread Man looked up, stopped, stepped up to the boy and pushed his nose right into his face. Tull was about to gently shove it to the side when the gelding took a deep breath and blew his nostrils out long and hard. The fine spray of snot mixed into the warm air should probably have disgusted Tull but the boy found himself oddly grateful for the comedy shower. He wiped his face with the sleeve of his jacket and then lifted his hand to lay his palm on the horse's forehead. Gingerbread Man lowered his head, let out a deeply satisfied grunt and began walking towards the middle of the school. He found a spot to his liking and started pawing the ground. The horse looked expectantly at Tull, waiting for the boy to detach the lead rope and step back before buckling at the knees. As Tull watched the old gentleman roll with all the delight of a young colt, this way and that, legs sticking into the air and treading invisible water while rubbing the base of his thin mane as hard into the sand as possible a sense of wellbeing took hold of the sadness and turned it into a moment of eternity.

Before Tull could grasp it more clearly, Liberty's voice called to him from the entrance.

"Hey, I'm done. Everyone else has gone home. If you're finished in here I'll show you how to wrap his leg."

~~~

Her fingers were so nimble and quick that Tull had to cup her wrapping hand a couple of times to slow her down. Each time a surge went through him and he couldn't help but wonder why now but not earlier in the day when she'd held his hand in reassurance. Then there had been warm comfort in her touch but now, reaching for her as they crouched beside one another by the hind leg of an astonishingly well behaved Gingerbread

Man, suddenly there was desire again and though there was pleasure in the current he didn't really want it. He wanted it to stop. He'd accepted her disinterest in him in that way and he loved her friendship too much to have his stupid heart spoil it. But there was also that weird magnetism again, the skin on the back of her fingers seemingly nestling against his palm whenever they met.

He kept willing his heart to listen to his head but the stupid thing just wouldn't play ball. It revelled in her nearness, skipping along to its own excited beat.

He sighed deeply.

Liberty finished up the wrap and looked at him with kind eyes.

"Rough day, huh? Charity days. They leave us all a bit emotional. Don't worry you'll get the hang of it soon enough."

They rose to their feet, still holding each others gaze. In the periphery of his vision, in the tiny edge that was not filled by the green of her eyes, he saw her swallow. The urge to kiss her was almost overwhelming. For the first time in his life he understood those rough men in the old movies, the cowboys that just forcefully grabbed the dame of their choice and pressed violent kisses onto her lips. Only he didn't want force, he longed to nibble along the jagged edges of her mouth tenderly, wanted to kiss her softly until she'd let him do it over and over again.

"You're blushing," she stated with an amused smile.

Just then the office door opened.

"Liberty, put the oaf away for us, will you? Tull, come in, please. I want to have a word."

~~~

The office was a tiny, windowless room sparsely furnished with a desk, a phone, a filing cabinet, two chairs, a kettle and no frippery.

Lisa gestured to the visitor's chair for the boy to sit down, shut the door, weaved sideways around the table and then followed suit. She poured a measure of whiskey into a mug in front of her from a half empty bottle on the table. Her eyes followed Tull's and she grinned.

"Don't worry, I haven't drunk all of that tonight. This is only my second. Do you want one?"

Tull shook his head, "I'm not eighteen yet."

Lisa shrugged and scrunched up her face, "Who cares? What you did today most adults shy away from and it's well deserving of a Scotch – *if* you want one."

"No thanks."

"Hmm," Lisa put the mug to her lips and took a sip, "Funny boy, you are," she mumbled over the rim, "It took me a while to click but I remember you."

She took a proper mouthful of the liquid and swallowed it down before lowering the mug back onto the table.

"You're the boy from Grange Avenue. You used to come running out of the house and pet the horses every time we rode by."

It was a statement, not a question, and Tull didn't see the need to respond. He waited for her to continue. She nodded at the bottom of her mug.

"Once I twigged it was obvious. Christine always reckoned you would show up at the yard one day," she looked up, "So I suppose you could say I've been waiting for you."

She paused for a long time, picking up a coin that was lying on the table and twirling it between her fingers.

"So," she carried on at long last, "Liberty says you want to learn to ride. Is that right?"

Tull stopped breathing for a moment then gathered his wits.

"Yes," he answered under his breath, "more than anything."

Lisa smiled and nodded silently for a while.

"Well, then I guess we should find you something a little bigger than Titch," she winked at him, "How would the Gingerbread Man suit you to start with? I know he's a bit stiff some days but he always needs gentle exercise and there isn't a kinder schoolmaster on the yard. I could give you a proper lesson twice a week. Tuesdays and Thursdays would work for me and once you've had a few and know how to tack up, you can always take him in the school without me shouting at you. Just walk him around a bit and practice your weight aids. In return I expect you to keep doing what you have been doing. It's been good for Liberty to have help. She does too much around here and I rely too much on her. I know that," she finished her drink and reached for the bottle to pour another, "But do you know how many girls like her are out there?"

She fixed him with her eyes as if it was a serious question and Tull couldn't help but respond.

"One?" he enquired with mild sarcasm.

"That's exactly right," Lisa answered earnestly, "One. Don't get me wrong, I get at least a girlie a month that shows up offering work for lessons but none of them lasts. As soon as they realise it's not just a bit of grooming or they meet a boy they vanish again. No dedication left in the world, I tell you. But Liberty? Now there is a proper grafter.

Never complains, always reliable. She's been with me since she was yay high," Lisa held her hand up to about 5 feet off the floor, "Little scrawny, scruffy thing turns up one day, pretty much mute and just starts chipping in. Doesn't ask for anything just *works*. And she's still here. Six years later. Amazing. Absolutely, bloomin' amazing. But she could do with some slack. I know that. Especially with her exams coming up next year. I know she wants to do well, even if she has a place guaranteed in the best equine college in the country already. I know she wants to stick two fingers up to all those idiots who thought she was stupid. And I want her to have that. So," she took a deep breath, "What do you say?"

"Yes, please, thank you very much?" Tull suggested.

He was too astonished to remain altogether serious. It seemed too wondrous, too easy.

"There are two provisos," Lisa continued, happily slurping her whiskey, "You need to go and buy your own hat. That's the only expense I expect you to fork out for. Secondly, I don't want any teenage drama on the yard. So you keep your hands off the girls here. It's hard enough keeping them from scratching each others' eyes out over horse stuff, I dread to think what would happen if the boy pin up started going out with one of them.

So they're strictly off limits," she rose to her feet and extended her hand across the desk, "Agreed?"

Tull stood up and looked at the offered hand.

It had been a long day.

It had brought him to the brink of what he could handle and right back again.

He thought of Jessica's eyes when she'd asked him if he thought she was pretty, of leading Titch through the forest in the winter twilight, of Victoria too weak to carry on the ride, of Gingerbread Man rolling around in the sand and of Liberty, strong and dependable throughout, beautiful, kind and maybe, just maybe, not quite as unattainable as he'd thought.

He shook his head.

"I'm sorry," he whispered, "I can't."

He left quickly and shut the door quietly on the way out.

~~~

The stable block was empty. Liberty had evidently left without him and as he walked slowly down the aisle towards the doors, listening to the horses shuffling in their boxes, he thought it was befitting to be doing this on his own. He'd entered alone, he would exit the same.

He picked up the pace and his hectic steps drowned out the suppressed sound coming from Oliver's box, the last on the right. One hand already on the door that would spit him back out into a horseless world, he stopped for a moment and suddenly heard it.

Someone was crying. Surreptitiously and as quietly as humanly possible.

He turned back and stepped up to the cob's stable. On the other side of the pony he saw Liberty sitting in the far corner, knees drawn up and forehead resting on them as ripple after ripple of silent tears shook her body.

Tull pushed the bolt on the door to the side and entered the box. Oliver let off his hay net for a moment and looked at the boy, blew out his nose then returned to the task of eating. Tull pushed the pony's neck up enough to dive under to the other side and crouched down in front of the girl. Liberty who had glanced up at him during the manoeuvre was now wiping her face with her sleeve.

"Hey," she grinned, her tone all 'fancy meeting you here' and 'I haven't been sobbing my heart out, honest'.

Tull frowned, "I can see the tears, Liberty."

She grinned harder, "You need to get your eyesight checked. No bawling happening around here," she sniffled, "I need a tissue. – What did Lisa want?"

Tull sat back on his haunches and shuffled around to her side, back against the stable wall. He looked down at himself. Underneath his jacket and jumper he was wearing his favourite T-shirt. It was nothing terribly special, just plain white with long black and white striped sleeves, thinned and softened from a million washes but he loved it. He sighed, dug under his layers, grabbed the hem and bit it with his incisors until he got the beginnings of a tear. He tore out a not very square piece, smoothed the rest of his clothing back into place and handed the scrap of fabric to Liberty.

"Here."

She took it wide-eyed and stared at it for a moment, "Thanks. You could have just got me some loo roll from the toilet, you know."

He shrugged and looked politely ahead into the space between the cob's sturdy legs while she blew her nose. When she was finished she nudged his shoulder with her own.

"Go on. Spill. What did she say?"

"She offered me lessons on Gingerbread Man," he answered hollowly, still staring at the underside of Oliver's belly.

Liberty turned her head to face his profile and although technically not meeting her eyes he knew she was frowning. Frown number 48: 'What on earth?!?'

"That's great, Tull," she said somewhat unsurely, "It's what you've always wanted, isn't it? Don't let the sadness of today spoil it for you. Be happy. It's a great opportunity."

He breathed out, long and audibly.

"I didn't take her up on it," he let the back of his head roll sideways along the cold wall to face her. She was only inches away from him and he could see her pupils inflate in the changing light.

"Are you insane? Why ever not?" Her head and shoulders shook in disbelief but then he fixed her with his eyes again and suddenly she became very still.

"The price was too high," he answered softly.

She sucked in her cheeks, "Keep talking."

He swallowed.

"She wanted me to promise that I keep my mitts off the girls here," he paused, "including you," he put a hand up to stop her from cutting in, "Yes, I know, don't say it. Cause you know what? It actually stings every time you do. But I live in hope, Liberty. I figure there are other horses and other yards. I'm not ten anymore. I'm working now and I've been saving up for my driving licence and a car, so I can get myself places. Somebody else, somewhere else might be willing to swap help for lessons or else once I've got a car and insurance and all that I can probably pay for them. Whatever, the point is I couldn't promise Lisa what she asked for because," he looked away, not being able to meet her eyes for the next part, "I'm still hoping you might change your mind about your type one day."

He glanced back tentatively, heat rising in his cheeks. She was staring at him transfixed and for a moment he wondered whether she'd heard any of it. Slowly she seemed to thaw from her state of shock.

"You idiot! You turned her offer down for *me*?"

He nodded and she turned her face away to stare ahead. They sat in silence for a long time, Liberty occasionally shaking her head at the empty space in front of her nose.

"What if," she finally said, "I did change my mind and then you found out that I'm a complete disappointment as a girlfriend. – Oh you silly boy! You should have gone for the horse! Horse trumps girl any day."

He smiled into the air, "Not this girl."
She shot him a sceptical side glance then begun kneading her hands nervously.

"You know," she mumbled, "I've never been kissed by anyone, ever. Not by a single soul. Not even my parents. You know how other parents kiss their children goodnight? Not mine. Not in my house. Not ever. I know it's not practice for kissing a boy but I mean *never*. What if my lips don't work that way? What if, you know, I *can't*."

Tull saw tears gathering in her eyes again and for one moment he forgot his awe. He reached for her and pulled her close by the nape of neck, raising his other hand to wipe the tears away with his thumb. Her skin was so soft that for one irrational second he feared his rough hands, so much like hers now, would lacerate it.

"Shut your eyes," he demanded quietly.

"Tull, I…"

She seemed so frightened it felt like his heart was being torn out.

"Just this once. For me. Please, Liberty. This *I* can do. Trust me."

She took a deep breath as if she needed to brace herself then shut her eyes and melted against his palm in her neck. He watched her face for a fraction of a second, wanting to burn it to memory for the rest of his life.

Finally, he let his lips meet hers.

There was no denying they were different, textured and harder than his at the top but soft and supple at the bottom. The contrast drove him spare with desire for more instantly.

He kissed her once, twice, a third time and was about to force himself to stop when suddenly she kissed him back. Gently testing, she responded to his lips with equal tenderness and he heard himself groan as he almost doubled over with the rush.

She opened her eyes.

"Are you okay?" she mumbled against his lips.

"Yes. No. We need to stop here or I'll just want more, Liberty, way way way more," he answered truthfully.

She smiled, still lips against lips, "They work alright then?"

"Yup," he breathed, "plenty fine."

"Great," her mouth sought his again, bolder now, a little surer, "Define more."

Suddenly this was easy.

"Everything," he drew back and began stroking her face, "I want to walk to school with you. I want to sit with you at lunch. I want to cook for you and if Lisa will still let me, I want to watch you ride sometimes. Just be with you. All of it."

There was a glint in her eyes he'd never seen before and it went straight to his pulse.

"More kissing?" she asked.

"I hope so," he answered and ran a finger along her lips.

"Then show me more," she smiled, "Way, way, way more."

Just then, Oliver shuffled around in the stable to push his nose down in between the two people taking up room on his bed. They both looked at the cob and Liberty laughed, already rising to her feet.

"But maybe not here," she dusted herself off while Tull slowly got up, "Come."

She patted her pony good night and they left the box.

Standing in the aisle she grabbed Tull by the shoulders, every inch confident Liberty again, tall and proud.

"Wait here, don't go anywhere. I'll be back in a second."

She turned abruptly and made her way towards the office.

It seemed as if as soon as Tull had seen her knock and enter he saw her come out again, her face inscrutable. When she got back to him she grinned, slipped her hand into his and started dragging him towards the doors.

"Right, back on track. Same work load as before, lessons twice a week. Your first one is this Tuesday. You better get yourself a hat before then because I know from experience that *that* part is *not* negotiable. - Now, this ratatouille you mentioned some time back, how quickly can you knock one up? I'm starving."

She didn't retract her hand the entire way home.

★

Katharina Marcus

Eleanor McGraw, a pony named Mouse and a boy called Fire

If you liked this short novella you might also enjoy Katharina Marcus' previously published full length novel *Eleanor McGraw, a pony named Mouse and a boy called Fire.*

Eleanor McGraw, vertically challenged, empathic and sharp daughter of folk musician Isabel Payne and a world famous rock guitarist, wakes up to a life more ordinary.
After years of vagabonding around the world alongside a series of chaotic father figures, they are settling down with quiet Kjell, a Swedish dentist, on the outskirts of a small town on the South coast of England. While exploring her new surroundings, Eleanor discovers a solitary pony in a deserted plot of grazing land.
As she befriends the animal and meets scar-faced, foul-mouthed Pike she is slowly drawn into another family's tragic past and finds herself at the centre of a decision between life or death, past or future, beginning or end.

"I was utterly entranced by this story from the first page. You could describe it as a story of awakening, of first love, a pony story, a coming of age story, a story of mixed and broken families. It's all of these and so much more." – **Cheyenne Blue, author and editor**

"This book is a cracking read, from an author who's not afraid to tackle what it's really like being a teenager." – **Jane Badger, author of 'Heroines on Horseback', reviewer and blogger**

"Life-affirming, poignant and profound, this book is written with a very apparent love for language; it entertains from the very first page to the last, with a real puzzle at its heart that is not solved for the reader until the very end." – **MariaJ, Amazon reviewer**

Paperback available at Amazon, thebookdepository and many other retailers. Ebook available at Amazon.

Chapter 1

For a fraction within eternity she didn't know who, what or where she was. She was floating in a soup of grey, wondering whether she was an embryo in a womb or a mammoth tree, a thousand years old.

With the question of age came the realisation that she was a who, not a what, and with the who came a name.

Eleanor.

My name is Eleanor.

I am a human.

I am 13 years old.

I am in bed.

It's supposed to be my bed but it smells wrong.

It doesn't smell like home. It smells of paint. And dentist.

If I open my eyes (but I don't want to) I will see white walls, thick yellow curtains (a gift from Granny), a perfectly polished wooden floor, a dark red rug (still not sure about the colour), a brand new wardrobe (which I chose), a brand new desk (which I chose) and my old rickety desk lamp (which I love). There are two unpacked boxes of books at the foot of the bed and an unassembled bookshelf leaning against the wall (can't be bothered). I...

There was a gentle tap on the door and suddenly she knew that this was the second knock.

It had been the first one, a while back, which had dragged her into consciousness through that opaque liquid of raw thought matter. Still, she didn't react.

She kept her eyes closed and looked through the door from behind her eyelids. She could see Kjell's silhouette standing patiently on the other side. He waited for another few seconds for her to answer then silently moved off.

This was what set this man apart from the Jerrys, Micks and Lukes of this world. The JMLs would have just walked in anyway or, most likely, not knocked in the first place.

Eleanor liked him for this. For the respect he showed her and the quiet reassurance, with which he went about his day.

'Shame,' she heard her grandmother giggle in the ether, *'it comes with such utter dullness.'*

She was beginning to find it difficult to keep her eyes shut now. She took a deep breath and opened them.

It was odd.

Everything was just as she had seen it from inside her skull yet somehow, in reality, it wasn't half as stark. The sun fell through the curtains and the whole room was bathed in a golden glow. There was her amply furnished pin board above her desk opposite the bed and pictures up, which they had hung the night before, along with the guitar swing that was now waiting for her to liberate the instrument from its travel case.

It was alright.

There was a noise from under the door and she turned her head to see an envelope being pushed into the room.

A beat, shuffling footsteps, then murmuring voices on the landing. A kiss *(did she actually hear that or just imagine it?)*, heavy footsteps back to the master bedroom and lighter ones down the stairs, carrying a suitcase. The front door opened and shut.

She really needed a pee now but didn't want her mother to find out she was awake and had chosen not to say goodbye.

Why, anyway? Why didn't I just go and say bye? He's off to Sweden for a fu-ne-ral, for heaven's sake.

It was a rhetorical question that didn't even sound like her own voice in her head. She knew the answer. It lay somewhere between feeling awkward around this softly spoken, intelligent and successful foreigner and being the outsider to an emerging bubble of a happy, brand new life.

A remnant of old.

A child of the JMLs.

Chapter 2

"So, what shall we do with our Thursday then? How do you fancy a bike ride to those fields we saw from the car the other day and explore the countryside around here? Or we could cycle to the beach and eat ice cream."

Her mum was propped up in bed, balancing a mug of Ovaltine on her enormous belly. Eleanor gave her a sceptical look.

"Are you sure you should still be riding a bike, mum? Our baby is due in five weeks, two days and Kjell would kill me if something happened to you two while he's gone. If he had his way you'd stay right where you are and I'd wait on you hand and foot. And I'm not sure he doesn't have a point."

Her mum laughed.

"Firstly, *my* baby is due in five weeks and two days, *your* little brother or sister. I didn't realise you were counting, by the way, that's cute. And secondly, like you quite rightly pointed out, Kjell is not here. Seriously," she dropped her voice and looked straight at Eleanor, her often unsteady hazel eyes suddenly focusing sharply, "I'll be fine. - Why? What was in that envelope?"

"A death threat," Eleanor dead-panned, "No, a load of cash for me to use for cabs and stuff in an emergency and a whole list of phone numbers where I can call him should I not get through on his mobile. He's worried, mum. Why is he so worried?"

Her mum laughed again, running her free hand through the mass of shaggy dark brown hair she was forever trying to smooth down with little success. She held it in the nape of her neck, arm resting on her head, as she sighed deeply, while her gaze wandered to just above Eleanor's shoulder, staring into the distance beyond the walls.

"He's not worried, babe, he's being practical," a wry smile spread across her face before her eyes fixed on Eleanor again, "There are lots of men like that. It's just that he's the first one of those you have met, thanks to my appalling track record. Also, it's his first child. It's different for him."

"What do you mean?"

"Well, I got all my fretting out of my system with you and now I know that a child can be so skinny and tiny it disappears when you shut one eye, yet still navigate safely through all sorts of chaos and make it to nearly fourteen relatively unharmed."

"Hm."

Eleanor had only been half listening and had dropped her head to start cleaning imaginary dirt from under her fingernails. Isabel sipped on her drink, searching her daughter's forehead over the rim of the mug.

"What do you mean 'hm'?"

"Nothing. - Just hm. So, you sure about this bike ride?"

"Yep."

"Ok. Bike ride then," Eleanor looked up again, "But I vote countryside. There is only so much beach and ice cream I can handle in one week."

"Shame. I was looking forward to the ice cream part," Isabel released her hair and shuffled into a more upright position, "Now what's the 'hm' about?"

Eleanor could feel her mum probing around in her brain and sighed because she knew, she knew and wouldn't let it go.

"It's about Monday, isn't it? You're anxious. - Look, we can postpone you going there till after the holidays, if you like. Settle in a bit more. Get your bearings. You finished your year in Gloucester. You don't have to go back to school here now, just have an extra week's holiday," she finished on a laugh, "I would."

Yes, I know. But chances of me suddenly growing a foot or so over the summer and putting on a stone or two are pretty slim (no pun intended), so why bother? Might as well get it over and done with now.

She didn't say it though. She didn't want to discuss it. So she shook her head in a deliberately absentminded fashion, knowing full well it wouldn't wash with her mum but hoping that she would accept the farce for what it was and let her change the subject.

"Mum, do you miss Gloucester? Do you miss our - chaos?" Eleanor asked.

"Not yet, no. Do you?"

"Maybe. I don't know. Everything is so, so, so tidy in this house. And everything smells of dentist all the time. It doesn't feel like home. I miss my bed, I miss the colours. I miss the smell of other people."

"Roll ups and beer you mean? Come here, gimme a cuddle," her mum's face went soft and serious as she put her arm around Eleanor and kissed her on the top of the head, "hmm, sprite hair, lovely. – Look, if you want to paint your walls pea green with orange and canary yellow zebra stripes, feel free. If you want to get rid of the bed and put a mattress on the floor, feel free. This is your house, too," after a moment she added with a grin, "If you want to start smoking and drinking though don't feel free, feel decidedly unfree and shackled."

Eleanor ignored the last remark.

"No, it's not. It's Kjell's."

"No, it's *our* house. In very real terms, we bought it together."

"But he picked it," Eleanor found herself arguing *(why am I even going on about this?)*, "he's been living here for months."

"Only so you didn't have to change schools half way through the year, hon," her mum's voice took on a no-nonsense, mildly annoyed tone, "A lot of this move has revolved around you and your feelings, Eleanor. We've tried to do it all as smoothly as possible for your benefit, you know."

It didn't revolve around my feelings! It revolved around what you assumed my feelings would be! We 'discussed' it but you never actually asked outright! And anyway since when do you care about taking me out of school half way through the year?!

Although screaming inside, Eleanor knew that it was up to her how the rest of this day would go and she didn't want to have a row. Instead, she snuggled into the hug again, snaking around the big belly between them and stated quietly, "I'm sorry. It's just, I think part of me misses them, you know. And I keep thinking, so must you. - It's so terribly, terribly quiet in this house."

"Sorry, you lost me, miss who?"

Her mum looked genuinely puzzled.

"Nobody," Eleanor sighed, "The JMLs."

"The what?"

"The Jerrys, Micks and Lukes of this world."

Suddenly the mount of flesh next to her started trembling and then bouncing wildly until she was practically catapulted out of the hug. She sat upright and looked at her mum wide-eyed.

Her mum was laughing so hard, tears had formed in the corners of her eyes. Once she had calmed down a little, her eyes narrowed and she looked inquisitively into Eleanor's.

"Ok, who came up with that? You or your grandma? Be honest."

Eleanor swallowed.

"Part part. I shortened it."

Her mum drew a long breath.

"Right. Now. Listen. You're that age now - so if you remember nothing else, remember this: the JMLs," another giggle escaped Isabel's lips before she could continue, "of this world, the rock stars with the bikes and the guitars and the pet wood lice and the tattoos and the wild imagination and the music that burns itself into your soul and the words that never leave, they

are fantastic fun and I don't regret a single day spent with any of them, particularly with your father. But you know, they are also incredibly self involved. It is all about them. About *their* chaos and *their* joy and *their* pain and *their* soul searches and *their* creativity and *their* self esteem or lack thereof. About what *they* want to eat and what *they* want to listen to and what *they* want to do next. I know your Grandma thinks, Kjell is boring. And I know you find him awkward because he doesn't come with this perpetual noise level that seems to have emanated from your collective father figures so far. But the fact is, for the first time in about twenty years, I am actually getting my own stuff done. And for the first time in my *life* I have somebody who calls me Isabel – not Izzy, not Bizzy, not Bella, not Lala, not Bumblebee but Isabel. I've got somebody who is genuinely interested in how I'm progressing with what I'm doing, who lets me breathe my own breaths and who wouldn't care if I was more successful than him. And not because he doesn't have his own things going on and needs to live through me, either. I've had that one before, too. No, because he is content enough in his own skin to let me be. I don't know whether you understand any of this yet but, look, go over to that chest of drawers and open the bottom drawer for me." Eleanor did as requested. "Now take out the black folder at the top and bring it here."

When Eleanor arrived back at the bed, her mum grabbed the folder and opened it. She took out some sheets of paper and shoved them into Eleanor's hands.

"Take a peek."

Eleanor found herself looking at music, handwritten in her mum's unmistakable stroke. As her eyes moved along the notes she started hearing a sweet, slow melody in her head – an intro to something bigger and breathtaking yet distinctly simple.

"Wow, mum, I didn't realise you started composing again. This sounds great. Very sweet. When did you start doing this? What is it going to be?"

Isabel shrugged.

"To be honest, I'm not sure what it wants to be. I've been playing other people's music for so long.... I don't know. I think it might be for your brother or sister. Like *Kittens in the Den* was for you. Although this one," she poked her belly lovingly with a finger, "doesn't appear to be half as talented as you were. Seems more interested in sleeping and eating than composing. But that isn't the point. The point is, I started when we got here," she looked at Eleanor almost imploringly, "Somehow, this, Kjell, the silence, it works for me, you see? It's like, like I can finally hear my own notes again," she took the sheets from Eleanor and shuffled to get up, "Now, can we go cycling or is this conversation some elaborate ploy to keep me in bed after all? Let's roll."

Chapter 3

They had only been going for about ten minutes when Eleanor heard her mum holler from behind to stop.

When she did and turned around she immediately started to regret having accepted the bike ride idea.

The exercise in the sweltering late morning heat had turned the walrus that was her heavily pregnant mother into a bright red blob creature, panting heavily and dripping with sweat.

"I need a rest, hon, I'm sorry."

Isabel got off her bike. She let it rest against a fence, took her helmet off, leant forward and lifted her shirt to mop her face, exposing the taut belly underneath. Just then, the baby decided to move and Eleanor could see it shifting under the skin. It made her heart quicken with a sudden jolt of anxiety and she began looking around frantically for a place where her mum could sit and rest in the shade for a bit.

They knew from the expedition earlier in the week that the road they were on was the main road into nowhere. There were a few more detached dwellings with manicured lawns on either side, then an open green on the right opposite a long, impenetrable and unkempt hedge of seven foot high bramble, elderberry and rosehip bushes, which had been fenced in with 'Private' signs nailed to the fence at regular intervals. Beyond that, where civilisation truly stopped, the road led through a small wooded area, on the other side of which were open fields and eventually a farm.

The wooded area had been where they had been headed but looking at her mum now, Eleanor was tempted to just walk up to the front door of any of the guaranteed-to-own-a-teapot houses and ask to utilise their gazebo. The scene in her mind made her giggle and her mum, who'd progressed to sipping water from a bottle now, frowned at her inquisitively. Eleanor waved off the question and looked around again. There appeared to be a shady gap between the 'Private' fence line and the flint stone wall encompassing the house just before it.

Eleanor squinted at it.

"Look mum, I think there is a twitten that goes up there. Let's see whether we can find a nice tree stump or something for you to sit on."

They pushed their bikes across the road and entered the path. Although the entrance was obscured by low hanging branches, once passed, the twitten turned out to be surprisingly wide. It was lined on one side by the same hedge that ran along the main road and on the other by the continuation of the flint stone wall, in front of which stood some sweet chestnut trees interlaced with hazels and shrubs, creating a dark, cool corridor under a canopy of leafy green.

Coming out of the glaring sun, both their eyes and bodies had to adjust and Eleanor felt a couple of shivers ripple through her body. They were only subtle but rather than ebb away, they seemed to lodge themselves in a state of suspended animation somewhere deep inside between her stomach and hips. They stayed there as she pushed on up the path, trying to ignore the very clear feeling that the decision to go in here had been one of those moments in life when it really *did* matter whether you went left or right. And she had no idea, whether in a good or a bad way.

Her mother, however, left no doubt as to her feelings about getting out of the sun and into the shade and kept making appreciative noises.

"Oh, this is much better. Well spotted, Eleanor. Oh look, there is actually a bench! How perfect is that?"

Only now did Eleanor notice a gap in the hedgerow ahead, making space for a long metal gate. Opposite the gate somebody had indeed dumped a park bench under a tree. Her mum's legs suddenly went into overtime as she pushed past Eleanor and hurried towards it. She wedged her bike between the wall and a tree and flopped down, stretching out her feet.

"Ahhh," she exhaled, "wake me when it's home time."

Eleanor followed her slowly, wondering not for the first time in her life, how it could possibly be that two people in the same place at the same time could perceive it so utterly differently. While her mum had clearly found an oasis of rest, in which all that was lacking was a handsome man feeding her grapes and massaging her feet, all Eleanor could feel was overwhelming loneliness seeping through the cool air. She felt almost as if she was back in the grey soup of pre-consciousness that had marked the beginning of this day, although this time the question was not who or what she was but *why* she was *still here*. Why she had not been taken *(where?)* with the others *(who?)*. Amidst this strange sense of devastation, a fragment of a song that Jerry had used to play for her when she was little came into her head: *'There is no treasure left here; no joy no light, no gold; what once was bright and beautiful; is withered now and old; so don't go looking further, just turn around and run; back to the beginning, to where you started from.'*

Only she *couldn't* turn around.

Pulled along by an invisible thread, yet somehow dragged against the tide, she felt as if she was wading through treacle and if she had had to run, she wouldn't have been able to. The idea terrified her and she tried to calm herself by silently singing the lines again in her head. The attempt backfired because then, for a moment, she wasn't sure anymore whether she had maybe heard the music for real, ever so faintly, in the distance and that freaked her out even more.

When she finally sat down next to her mum on the bench, it felt like it had taken hours to get there.

"This is not a good place, mum. I don't like it. I reckon we should go back as soon as you can. Go home, have some ice tea, no more adventures."

"Teenagers," her mum mumbled, "you're so sensitive. - Why can't you just ignore the vibe and chill?" She opened her eyes and stared ahead at the metal gate. "We'll go in a minute. It does taste rather of sadness around here. – What do you reckon is in there?"

Eleanor shrugged.

"Something private," she answered dryly before getting up to have a look.

As she approached the gate, she knew that she was edging towards the source of whatever it was that was hanging in the air but strangely that came as a relief. With every step closer the feeling became less hers and more that of what lay beyond. She was half expecting to find an old cemetery and was genuinely surprised and mildly disappointed to find an empty plot of grazing land instead, the other side of which was not discernable from this vantage point.

"It's just an empty field, mum. I guess it normally has cows or sheep in it, I can see a barn or something."

"Not a cemetery then? Hm," Isabel grunted over from the bench.

Eleanor smiled and was about to turn back when suddenly there was a movement quite close to her, in the hedgerow adjoining the other side of the gate. She stepped onto the bottom rung to lean over - and suddenly found herself eye to eye with a pony.

It was small, a funny kind of blue-grey colour and was watching Eleanor with sorrowful eyes. As soon as Eleanor looked into them, she knew that she was facing the owner and occupant of that wasteland of grief she had just trudged through up the path.

"Hello there," Eleanor whispered softly and stretched out a hand, "I'm Eleanor. Pleased to meet you."

The pony hesitated then slowly came forward to nuzzle the palm of Eleanor's hand with its soft mouth. It wasn't looking for a treat, just sniffing tenderly before stepping up even closer and blowing some warm air into the girl's face. Instinctively, Eleanor gently blew back and it made a low greeting sound in its throat.

Just then, Isabel heaved herself up from the bench, startling it and it turned to canter off, disappearing down into a part of the field Eleanor could not see from where she was.

"Oh mum, you spooked it!" she exclaimed disappointedly and looked at her hand, "That was amazing."

"Spooked what?" Isabel frowned as she approached.

"Did you not see it?"

"See what?"

"The pony."

Chapter 4

For the rest of the day Eleanor felt out of synch - like a person on screen when the sound lags behind the picture.

And every time she shut her eyes, there it was again.

The pony.

Looking at her with those eyes.

It had all been so surreal.

By supper time she wasn't even sure anymore whether it had been real or a ghost and found herself repeatedly rubbing the palm of her hand where it had sniffed her; or blowing against it to feel her breath ricocheting back into her face, in a desperate attempt to recreate *that* moment.

Her mum seemed oblivious to Eleanor's state *(although one could never be sure with that woman)* and went to bed early, leaving Eleanor to pace the house, not knowing what to do with herself or where to settle.

When, after some hours of touring between television, computer, bookshelf and fridge, Eleanor finally found her bed the restlessness morphed into a fitful sleep, spiked with what the Dutch called spaghetti dreams, from which she woke every half hour.

Peace, and with it some deeper sleep, finally came with a decision made just before dawn, on the way back from the toilet. She would get up early, before her mum, and go back there.

When she did find herself gently pulling the front door shut sometime in the paper round hours of the following morning that same peace turned into a continuously thumping heart as she felt the adrenaline pumping through her body. For a moment, she wanted to turn, go back into the house and scurry back to bed. But the idea of carrying on another day as restlessly as the night before seemed infinitely worse than the sheer fear of leaving a house she hardly called home to cycle around a forlorn part of a place she hardly knew and get lost on a twitten that potentially had wolves on it.

As she wheeled the bike out onto the empty road she was giving herself a well rehearsed lecture in the back of her mind on empty paths, rapists and strangers, while half visualising a funeral with herself in the starring role and her mum having an emergency Caesarian induced by the stress of burying her daughter.

Another, much more plausible, vision came to the front, showing her mum in bed right now, going into labour, calling for her with no reply.

She took a deep breath and pushed down on the pedals. She promised herself she would be quick and when she felt the cool air stream around her face it blew away all anxiety.

Without the walrus in tow and with the advantage of knowing the way now *(why was it that once you had gone a route before it always seemed shorter than the first time?)* it took her barely five minutes before she came to a halt in front of the entrance to the twitten. She could have cycled up to the metal gate but she thought it might frighten the pony *(if it was even there)* so she got off, locked the bike to the 'Private' fence and started walking.

The path seemed darker than the day before but also, today, it seemed like just a path. There was nothing of note hanging in the air, no vibe to pick up on. She was almost sure the pony wouldn't be there but she trudged on, fighting pre-emptive disappointment by concentrating on her body.

Exertion from the ride, lack of sleep, anticipation and fear had drained her mouth of all moisture and she swallowed hard a couple of times, trying to generate some saliva with little success. By the time she came to the metal gate, she felt entirely consumed by a need for water.

One look across told her she had been right. No pony. She was about to turn back when she saw a tap on a post next to a water trough, where the pony *(or ghost of a pony)* had been standing the day before.

She hesitated but the thirst won. Heart beating wildly, she climbed over the gate and within seconds found herself holding her head sideways under a cool stream of water, drinking in large gulps. Lost in the sensation of satisfying a burning need, she didn't hear the thundering hooves until she turned off the tap, by which time they were so near it made her spin around.

There it was, only a few feet away, dust whirling around its legs where they had stopped dead in their tracks. It was facing her, head and tail held high, pumping air through flaring nostrils, making short little snorting noises and looking at her with utter indignation.

It was as beautiful as it was impressive and for a moment Eleanor thought her heart was going to explode with admiration. She could feel herself tremble as she took a deep breath and stretched out a hand in a pacifying gesture.

"Hey there," she said in a low voice, "I'm sorry, I didn't mean to intrude. I was seriously thirsty, you see. I wouldn't normally just come in uninvited. I'm not that kind of person. I just needed a little drink." She could see the pony's stance relax with every word and carried on talking without moving. "I cycled really hard to get here.

I wanted to come see you. I'm not sure you remember me. I came yesterday. You sniffed my hand?" Eleanor knew that to an observer she would probably appear like the pony version of a mad cat lady in the making but the fact was, it was working. As she rambled on in a low voice, telling the pony about how she had thought about it all night and that she was new to the area and that she was going to start school in a few days, its head and tail lowered, indignation gave way to curiosity and it took a step forward.

Eleanor's heart, which had also quietened, made a leap again and she, too, took a step forward. The pony turned its head left then right, looking at her through each eye individually, gave another little snort and took another step forward. Eleanor gave it a second, then followed suit. She had stopped talking now and was waiting quietly for the pony to take another step. When it did, so did Eleanor. It felt a bit like a court dance out of some period drama. They were quite close now and Eleanor knew with the next step they would be within touching distance. She waited patiently for the pony to make another move.

Suddenly something rustled in the bushes. Eleanor jumped out of her skin but the pony didn't seem bothered at all. It looked in the direction of the noise, making a low sound in its throat before its eyes and head seemed to trace something moving behind the hedgerow, down to the road. They came back to rest their gaze on Eleanor, almost mocking now, as if to say *'you are a bit of a scaredy cat, aren't you?'* - And then it just sauntered over to her as if the whole dance had been nothing but a game between old friends, gave her a gentle nudge in the rib cage with its nose and began lightly rubbing its forehead against Eleanor's shoulder. Eleanor was so surprised and overwhelmed by the sudden show of affection, she didn't think twice about what to do next. She started circling her fingernails behind the pony's ears, which it seemed to enjoy a lot, and then she moved around it, making the same circling motion down its neck and along its body. When she had finished with the left side, the pony turned to offer up its right and Eleanor gladly obliged.

By the time she had finished, her fingertips were coated in a funny grey film of skin particles and grease that smelled intensely of horse. It should have grossed her out but instead she smelled it with pride. It was proof that the pony wasn't a ghost. It was real and it let her touch it - and right now it was giving her another nudge, this time as if to say *'come with me'*.

It started moving towards the gate and when Eleanor didn't immediately follow, it stopped and turned its head to look at her. Eleanor started walking and side by side they reached the gate.

A row of carrot pieces had been left on the top bar and the pony picked them off one by one. When it had munched through all of them, it turned back to Eleanor and looked at her expectantly, its soft lips gently, carefully air-nibbling at Eleanor's shirt. Eleanor laughed.

"No, I'm sorry, I didn't bring you any food. I wouldn't just feed somebody else's pet. I wouldn't normally be in here either. Although I think I might come and visit you again tomorrow. – I had better stay on the other side though, I have an inkling you are 'private' property."

Though she was trying to sound joky and light-hearted, as she heard herself say it, she could feel tears welling up in her eyes. The idea of not having that same closeness again made her choke. She slung her arms around the pony's neck and gave it a hug. The pony seemed to echo her sadness and leant its head against her back, gently pushing her into its chest, returning the embrace. She let herself sink into it and for a moment felt engulfed with strength, love and wisdom in a way she never had before.

"Goodbye," Eleanor whispered, then let go, turned, climbed the gate without looking back and ran down the path.

By the time she got back to her bike she was sobbing violently, hardly able to see. She fumbled with the key for a good few minutes, dropped it, picked it up again - until somewhere in the periphery of her blurred vision she clocked a small, old fashioned dark green motorbike by the side of the road, black helmeted rider aboard, engine running but stationary as he fuffed with his gloves.

There was something familiar and reassuring in that small detail of his hands opening and closing to get the fingers sitting just right in the leather, reminding her of both Mick and Luke. She felt another pang of loss but this one came with Mick's no-nonsense voice of road training her for her cycling proficiency.

'Stop being ridiculous. This is not safe. You can't even see the road. Now pull yourself together, dry those tears, get on your bike and go.'

Home.

Sleep.

Tomorrow (today) is another day.

Hope you enjoyed the excerpt.

Made in the USA
Columbia, SC
04 July 2017